The Pink Wall

By: John Louis Nagy

Copyright © 2026

John Louis Nagy

All Rights Reserved

The Pink Wall

By: John Louis Nagy

The Pink Wall

CHAPTER ONE

Brenda Holbul stood outside the glass doors like she was about to enter a whole new planet.

The building was bright and soft-looking from the outside—clean windows, pale pink signs, and a little logo of a ballerina silhouette posed on one toe. It didn't look scary.

But Brenda felt scared.

She adjusted the little straps on her ballerina uniform—soft white tights, pale pink slippers, a tiny skirt that felt like it could float away if she moved too fast. Her hair was pulled back and tight the way her mom insisted. No loose strands allowed. No chaos.

Her mom, Gloria Holbul, leaned down beside her and kissed her cheek.

"You're gonna do great," Gloria whispered. "Just be sweet, be quiet, and try."

Brenda nodded fast. Too fast. Like her head was trying to escape her body.

Gloria opened the door for her.

Inside, the air smelled like warm wood floors and perfume and something kind of powdery—like baby lotion. Brenda stepped into the dance school and instantly felt a wave of noise hit her.

Not loud noise.

Little girl noise.

The kind of noise that comes from excitement, shoes scuffing, tiny laughs, and everyone talking at once like they were born to fill the air.

There were twelve girls in the room.

All about Brenda's size. All in ballerina gear. All with their own little worlds in their eyes.

Brenda didn't know where to put her hands. She didn't know if she should smile. She didn't know if she should speak first.

So she did the safest thing in her entire five-year-old brain.

She stood still and watched.

The girls were a mix of everything.

Different skin tones. Different hair. Different energy.

Two of the girls were African American, both with big curly hair and bright, fearless eyes. One of them was spinning in place like she had magnets in her feet that kept her balanced. Her arms were smooth. Her face wasn't even serious.

She was smiling while she spun.

Like it was easy.

Three of the girls were Latina, and you could feel it in the way they moved—even when they weren't trying. They carried rhythm in their bones like it came installed.

One of them was doing something that definitely wasn't ballet.

It looked like a crip walk routine, all quick foot taps and little hops, like she had music playing in her head that nobody else could hear. The other girls watched her and giggled.

Nobody told her to stop.

They just let her dance.

And then Brenda noticed the bigger girl.

She was taller and wider than the others, and her face had a soft slope to it, like she was always halfway into a happy thought. Her blonde hair was in pigtails, and her cheeks were rosy.

She wore a drooling grin.

Not mean.

Not weird.

Just… innocent.

Brenda didn't know why, but seeing her made Brenda feel less afraid. Like even if you didn't fit perfectly, you could still be here.

And the last group of girls—six of them—were like little doll versions of ballerinas.

The "Barbie" ones.

Small, neat, shiny hair, clean uniforms, cute little faces.

Brenda realized quietly:

I'm one of them.

Brenda had dimples when she smiled. She'd seen adults react to that like it was magic. Like dimples made you more safe. More lovable. More special.

She didn't understand why it mattered.

But she knew it did.

So she kept it tucked away inside her like a secret advantage.

Still… Brenda didn't know how to move yet.

Not confidently.

Not like the spin girl.

Not like the dancing Latina girl.

Brenda felt like her arms were made out of stiff paper.

She felt like her feet were glued on wrong.

She felt like she was wearing her own body incorrectly.

And that was the real reason her mom had sent her here.

Not just to dance.

But to learn how to exist in herself.

A moment later, the door at the side of the room opened.

A woman entered.

Short.

Old.

Strong.

Her hair was gray, her bun was tight, and her posture was like she had a ruler inside her spine.

This was Doris.

The teacher.

She didn't smile big. She smiled small. Like she didn't waste emotion, she used it carefully.

Doris walked straight into the room and clapped once—sharp and simple.

"Ladies."

Instantly, the room calmed down a little.

Not fully.

But enough.

Doris held a clipboard and started inspecting.

She went girl to girl, checking uniforms, looking at hair, fixing tiny mistakes like she'd done it a thousand times.

All the girls were tied up perfect.

Except one.

One of the Barbie-looking girls had dirty blonde hair and her straps were messed up, crossed wrong like a pretzel.

Doris didn't scold her.

She just crouched, fixed the straps, pulled them neat, and nodded.

"There," Doris said.

The girl looked relieved like she'd been saved from a disaster she didn't even understand.

Brenda stood frozen.

Doris finally looked up at the room again.

"Okay, girls," Doris said, voice calm but firm. "This is just day one."

The girls listened.

Even the one doing the crip walk stopped moving.

Doris continued.

"Day one is where you show up to prove to me you exist."

She paused, letting that land in their little brains.

"And you have heart."

Doris looked around slowly.

"Become acquainted. You are all like sisters now."

Brenda blinked.

Sisters?

She didn't know any of these girls.

But she liked the word.

It made her chest feel warm and safe.

Doris jotted something down on her clipboard, then lifted her eyes again.

"Okay. That's it."

The girls looked confused.

Doris pointed toward the exit.

"Go home. I'll see you ladies Wednesday. Do the stretches we discussed."

And just like that…

That was the whole day.

Brenda watched the girls begin shuffling toward the door, little slippers squeaking against the floor.

Some of them talked louder again as soon as Doris stopped speaking.

The spinning girl spun one more time for no reason.

The Latina girl bounced like she couldn't shut her energy off.

Brenda walked slowly, relieved she'd survived.

On the way out, the bigger girl with the pigtails caught Brenda's eyes.

She smiled wide.

A little drool fell from her mouth to the floor mid-smile.

She didn't notice.

Brenda smiled back anyway.

A small smile.

Dimple smile.

Then she stepped outside.

The sun felt brighter out there.

Like the world was saying, Okay. You did it.

Gloria's Astro Mini Van pulled up to the curb right on time.

Brenda climbed into the seat, buckled herself in, and stared forward like a soldier returning from battle.

Gloria glanced at her and smiled.

"Did you have a nice time, booboo?"

Brenda swallowed.

Then she nodded.

"Yes, mom. Thank you."

And the van rolled away, carrying Brenda Holbul into the beginning of something bigger than she could understand yet.

CHAPTER TWO

Wednesday came fast.

It didn't feel fast to grown-ups—grown-ups always thought days were slow and boring—but for Brenda Holbul, Wednesday came like a freight train.

Tuesday felt like one long nervous stomach ache.

She kept thinking about the room.
The wooden floor.
The mirrors.
The other girls moving around like they had invisible music pumping through their veins.

Brenda didn't have that.

Not yet.

And that was the scary part.

That morning, Gloria Holbul stood in the bathroom behind Brenda, holding a brush in one hand and a tired expression in the other.

"Hold still," Gloria said softly, but her voice had that edge in it—the edge of someone who had already been awake too long.

Brenda tried to hold still.

But her head tilted anyway.

Her hair was a little tangled.

Not dirty.

Not neglected.

Just… not salon-perfect like the girls on TV. And Gloria was doing her best, but "best" didn't always come out looking pretty when money was thin.

Gloria's hands moved quick.

She brushed, and brushed again.

Then tied Brenda's hair back, tight.

Brenda winced.

"Ow," she whispered.

Gloria froze, then loosened it just a tiny bit.

"Sorry, booboo," she said, kissing the top of Brenda's head. "We gotta keep it neat, okay? Doris is strict."

Brenda nodded even though she didn't fully understand what "strict" meant.

She only knew it meant:

mess up = shame.

mess up = attention.

mess up = everyone staring.

And Brenda did not want that.

Not yet.

The Astro Mini Van rattled like it always did.

The engine sounded like it was clearing its throat every time Gloria pressed the gas. The radio barely worked. One speaker was blown, so music came out sounding like a robot was drowning.

But Gloria still kept it clean inside.

Not fancy clean.

Just mom clean.

Brenda sat in the passenger seat like a tiny adult, her feet not even reaching the floor, hands folded in her lap.

Gloria glanced at her.

"You ready for day two?"

Brenda swallowed.

"I think so."

Gloria smiled and nodded, like that answer was enough to pay rent and fix the whole world.

"That's my girl."

They pulled up.

Bright building. Pink sign. Warm windows.

The same place as before.

But somehow… scarier now.

Day one had been a "heart check."

Day two was going to be work.

Inside, the twelve girls were already there again, scattered like glitter.

Some girls were stretching.

Some were chatting loud.

One girl spun again for no reason, just because spinning was her favorite thing in the universe.

Brenda stepped in and stayed near the wall like she belonged to the paint.

She noticed the African American girls first—the ones with the huge curly hair and energy that never died.

They were laughing at something funny.

They looked fearless.

Brenda wished she knew how to be fearless.

The Latina girls were dancing even when they weren't dancing.

It was like their feet never went fully still. Like music lived under their skin.

And then Brenda spotted Anastasia again—the bigger girl with the pigtails.

Anastasia wasn't doing anything fancy.

She was just standing there, smiling softly, like she was happy to be included in the room.

That made Brenda breathe easier.

Brenda didn't know why.

But it did.

Then the side door opened and Doris came in.

Same tight bun.

Same clipboard.

Same calm face like she was a judge and this was court.

Doris clapped once.

"Line up."

The girls scrambled into a crooked line fast, like little ducks trying to act military.

Brenda hurried too, trying not to be last.

She didn't want to stand out.

Doris walked down the line slowly, eyes sharp.

"Feet together," Doris said.

They pressed their feet together.

"Shoulders down."

They dropped their shoulders.

"Necks tall."

They stretched upward.

Brenda tried to copy exactly, but her body felt confused. Like it didn't speak the same language yet.

Doris paused by Brenda for just a second.

Not long.

But long enough for Brenda to feel like Doris could see straight through her.

"You," Doris said gently. "You're tense."

Brenda blinked.

Tense.

Was that bad?

Brenda whispered, "I'm sorry."

Doris shook her head.

"Don't apologize. Fix it."

The words weren't mean.

But they landed heavy.

Don't apologize. Fix it.

Brenda nodded like she'd just been given the most important secret in the world.

Doris walked to the front of the room and faced them.

"Today," Doris said, "we learn the basics. If you cannot do the basics, you will never do the fancy."

That made the girls go quiet.

Even the ones who always moved.

Doris stepped back and demonstrated.

"First position."

She turned her feet out, heels together, toes pointing out like a perfect little V.

Somehow she looked stable like a mountain even though her feet were turned wrong on purpose.

"Arms," Doris said. "Like you're holding a beach ball."

She lifted her arms into a soft circle.

"Not stiff," Doris warned. "Never stiff."

Brenda copied her.

Her arms shook a little.

Not because she was weak.

Because she wanted to be perfect so badly it made her nervous.

Doris paced the room.

"Chin up," she told one girl.

"Stop smiling like a clown," she told another.

"Your knees are locked," she said to a third.

Then she stopped at Brenda again.

Brenda's stomach dropped.

Doris crouched slightly.

"Your feet are not turned out enough," Doris said.

Brenda tried to twist them more.

It felt weird.

It hurt a little.

Doris nodded once, approving.

"Better."

That one word made Brenda's brain light up like fireworks.

Better.

Not perfect.

But better.

And better meant she was improving.

And improving meant she belonged.

After a few minutes, Doris clapped again.

"Now," Doris said. "We practice walking across the floor. Slow. Controlled. Like a queen. Like a swan."

One by one the girls walked.

Some girls were born with it—tiny posture, perfect arms, floating steps like they didn't weigh anything at all.

Some girls were clumsy.

Some were too loud.

Some stomped in slippers like they were wearing boots.

Then Brenda's turn came.

She stepped forward and walked slowly, arms raised like Doris showed.

And something strange happened.

She wasn't flashy.

She wasn't fast.

But she meant it.

Every step looked like it mattered.

Like she was stepping into a story.

Like she wasn't just walking, she was performing being brave.

Doris watched with a quiet expression.

Brenda reached the end of the floor and turned carefully.

She walked back.

Still controlled.

Still serious.

Still... intentional.

When she finished, she returned to the line.

And for the first time since she walked through the door...

Brenda felt proud.

Not loud proud.

Not bragging proud.

Just a private proud that warmed her bones.

The other girls began whispering.

Not mean whispers yet.

Not sharp.

But curious.

One of the Barbie girls glanced at Brenda's face.

Her dimples.

Her serious eyes.

Brenda caught the look.

And she remembered something she didn't have words for yet:

Sometimes other kids don't like you because you're bad.

But sometimes they don't like you because you're good.

Brenda didn't understand it fully.

But she felt it.

Doris finished the session with stretches.

"Hamstrings," she said.

The girls stretched.

Some giggled.

Some struggled.

Anastasia fell sideways and laughed, drool slipping down her smile again, and somehow it made everyone laugh too—not cruel laughter, just simple little-girl laughter.

Brenda laughed too.

And that was the first time Brenda felt like she wasn't alone.

At the end, Doris checked her clipboard again.

"All right," Doris announced. "You girls did fine."

Fine.

That word felt like a medal.

"Wednesday," Doris continued, "is discipline day. When you come here, you leave the outside world outside."

Some girls didn't even understand what she meant.

But Gloria would have.

Brenda would later.

Doris clapped once.

"You will practice at home. Ten minutes a day. Every day. No excuses."

The girls started collecting their tiny bags and water bottles.

Brenda walked toward the exit slowly.

She saw Anastasia again and gave her a small smile.

Anastasia smiled big back.

Brenda's dimples appeared.

And she didn't even try to hide them.

Gloria was waiting out front.

The Astro Mini Van idled like a sleepy beast.

Brenda climbed in.

Gloria looked her over like she always did—hair, uniform, face, posture.

"How'd it go?" Gloria asked.

Brenda sat up straight.

"Good."

Gloria smiled.

"You learn something?"

Brenda nodded.

Brenda's voice was small, but it carried something new inside it.

"Doris said… don't apologize. Fix it."

Gloria blinked.

For a moment she looked like she'd heard that sentence before in her own life.

Then she swallowed hard and smiled bigger.

"That's a good lesson," Gloria said. "That's a real one."

They drove away.

Brenda stared out the window as the dance school disappeared behind them.

She still felt nervous.

She still felt behind.

She still felt like everybody else had a secret book of instructions for being a ballerina…

…but she was learning.

And for Brenda Holbul…

learning was enough.

CHAPTER THREE

Brenda Holbul didn't sleep easy the night after Wednesday practice.

Not because she was scared of Doris.

Not because ballet was too hard.

But because her body felt different now.

Like it had been introduced to a new language.

Her legs ached in places she didn't know could ache. Her toes felt tired. Even her little shoulders felt like they'd been holding up invisible weight.

Brenda laid in her bed staring at the ceiling, thinking about the dance studio mirrors.

How they showed you everything.

How they didn't lie.

How you couldn't hide.

That part bothered her.

But another part of it made her feel… brave.

Like if she could face a mirror, she could face anything.

The next time Gloria dropped Brenda off, it was colder outside.

Gray morning.

The kind where the sky looks like it forgot how to smile.

Gloria tightened Brenda's coat around her and kissed her forehead.

"Go in," Gloria said. "You're gonna be okay."

Brenda nodded.

She walked up to the door and opened it herself this time.

Like a big girl.

Inside, the studio was already alive again.

Twelve little ballerinas, each one glowing in her own way.

Some girls were stretching, legs up on the barre like it was nothing.

Some were practicing little spins in front of the mirrors, checking their faces while they did it.

Because ballet wasn't just movement.

It was looking beautiful while you moved.

Brenda understood that already, and it bothered her a little.

Why did you have to look beautiful to be good?

Why couldn't you just be… real?

But Brenda didn't say anything.

She just stepped inside quietly and stood near the edge like she always did.

Watching.

Learning.

Trying to breathe like she belonged.

The two African American girls were there again, both loud and happy.

They were talking and laughing like they owned the whole room.

One of them, the one who always spun like gravity didn't apply to her, did a tiny twirl and clapped like she was congratulating herself.

The Latina girls were dancing again too—small hops, little side steps, rhythm leaking out of them even when they weren't trying.

Brenda watched them all and felt that old feeling creep in.

That feeling that everybody else knew how to live inside their body…

…and she was just visiting hers.

Then she saw the bigger girl again.

The one with the pigtails.

The one with the soft drooling grin.

She wasn't doing any fancy moves.

She was sitting on the floor near the wall with her legs stretched out, trying to touch her toes.

She wasn't doing very well at it.

But she was trying hard.

And she smiled the whole time.

Brenda didn't know why, but she liked that.

It felt honest.

Brenda looked around quickly.

Nobody was watching.

So Brenda did something brave.

She walked up to her.

Slow steps.

Quiet.

She stopped a few feet away.

The bigger girl looked up at Brenda with wide, friendly eyes.

She smiled.

A little drool slid down the corner of her mouth, shiny like a string.

Brenda didn't flinch.

She just smiled back with her dimples showing.

The bigger girl's smile got even wider.

"Hi," the bigger girl said. Her voice was a little thick, like her tongue was tired, but the word came out happy.

Brenda nodded. "Hi."

The bigger girl blinked at her for a second, like she couldn't remember what came next in conversations.

Then she pointed at Brenda.

"You… pretty."

Brenda's cheeks warmed.

She didn't know what to say to that.

So she said the first honest thing she could think of.

"Thank you."

The bigger girl nodded like that was the correct answer and then patted her own chest.

"I'm…" she paused, thinking hard.

Brenda leaned in a little, curious.

The girl's eyebrows scrunched. Her pigtails bounced when she moved her head like she was searching her brain for the right word.

Then she said it like she was proud of it:

"Anastasia."

Brenda stared at her.

It wasn't a common name like "Emily" or "Sarah."

It sounded like something from a storybook.

Something fancy and mysterious.

Something important.

Brenda smiled so wide her dimples deepened.

"Anastasia," Brenda repeated softly.

Anastasia nodded hard.

"Yes."

Brenda said, "That's a beautiful name."

Anastasia didn't fully understand the word beautiful the way grown-ups did, but she understood the tone.

She understood love.

So she giggled.

It sounded like bubbles.

Brenda sat down beside her without asking.

That was another brave thing.

And for the first time, Brenda didn't feel like she was the quiet girl in the corner.

She felt like she was part of something.

"Touch toes," Anastasia said, tapping her feet.

Brenda nodded. "Yeah."

Anastasia tried again, reaching forward with her hands and grunting a little.

She got close but not all the way.

Her face turned red.

She looked frustrated for half a second.

Then she laughed at herself.

And that laugh… it fixed everything.

Brenda tried too.

Brenda couldn't touch her toes either.

Not fully.

Her fingers were close, but her legs pulled tight like rubber bands.

She felt embarrassed for one second.

Then she remembered Anastasia laughing.

So Brenda smiled too.

"Hard," Brenda whispered.

Anastasia nodded fast.

"Hard," she agreed.

Then she leaned over like she was sharing a secret.

"Ballet hard."

Brenda giggled.

"Yeah."

A few of the other girls noticed Brenda sitting with Anastasia.

One of the Barbie girls wrinkled her nose like she was confused.

Like she couldn't understand why Brenda would choose that company.

The girls didn't say anything out loud.

Not yet.

But Brenda felt the shift.

That subtle thing kids do.

The invisible line.

The quiet judgment.

Brenda's stomach tightened.

But she didn't move away.

She didn't abandon Anastasia just because it might look weird.

Brenda stayed.

Because Brenda knew something even at five years old—

if somebody is kind to you, you don't trade them in for popularity.

The side door opened.

Doris entered.

Clap. One sharp sound.

"Ladies," Doris said.

The girls lined up quickly.

Brenda stood up and brushed imaginary dust off her skirt, then stood in line.

Anastasia waddled into place too, a little slow, but smiling the whole time.

Doris looked down the line like she was inspecting soldiers again.

"Good," she said. "Today, we build. We don't play."

That sentence made every girl go quiet.

Even the ones who liked to giggle.

Doris moved to the front of the room.

"First position."

The girls turned their feet out.

Brenda's feet didn't turn out as far as the others, but she tried.

And she remembered Doris's rule:

Don't apologize. Fix it.

So she adjusted.

Little by little.

Better.

Not perfect.

Better.

Doris paced the room.

She corrected arms.

She corrected shoulders.

She corrected chins.

She corrected posture.

Then Doris stopped again right in front of Brenda.

Brenda held her breath.

Doris studied her face for a second.

Her dimples weren't showing now because Brenda wasn't smiling.

Brenda was serious.

Focused.

Like she wanted it so bad it hurt.

Doris glanced down at Brenda's feet.

Then her arms.

Then her shoulders.

Doris nodded once.

"Conviction," Doris said.

Brenda blinked.

She didn't know what that word meant.

But it sounded like something powerful.

Doris said it louder, to the whole class:

"This one has conviction. You see it?"

Some of the girls looked at Brenda.

Brenda felt her cheeks burn.

She didn't want attention.

But Doris kept talking.

"She means what she does. That is rare."

Brenda's chest filled up.

Not with pride exactly.

With something more dangerous.

Hope.

Because hope made you believe you could win.

And winning in ballet meant other people would start looking at you differently.

Brenda glanced sideways at Anastasia.

Anastasia was struggling to keep her arms up.

They drooped a little.

She looked tired already.

But she was smiling.

Trying.

Brenda smiled at her softly.

And her dimples appeared.

Anastasia smiled back.

Drool glittered on her lip like a silly little jewel.

Brenda didn't care.

Doris clapped again.

"Across the floor," she commanded.

The girls took turns walking and stopping.

Walking and stopping.

Learning to move like ballerinas.

When Brenda's turn came again, she walked slow.

Strong.

Intentional.

She didn't bounce. She didn't rush. She didn't wobble.

She looked like she was taking each step with meaning.

Like she belonged on the floor.

Like she didn't need permission.

And some of the girls watched her with a tightness in their eyes.

It wasn't admiration.

Not fully.

It was the first spark of something else.

That quiet, savage childhood thing.

The thing that starts small.

Jealousy.

Competition.

The seed of Why her?

Brenda didn't notice it yet.

Not really.

Because Brenda was too busy trying to survive.

Trying to become herself.

Trying to earn her place in the room.

At the end of class, Doris clapped one last time.

"Good work," she said. "Go home. Stretch. Ten minutes. Every day."

The girls grabbed their things and started moving toward the exit.

Brenda walked beside Anastasia.

Anastasia held her little bag with both hands like it was heavy treasure.

Brenda said softly, "Bye, Anastasia."

Anastasia looked at her like Brenda had just gifted her the moon.

"Bye, Brenda," she said slowly, proud she remembered her name too.

Brenda's dimples appeared again.

And she walked out into the gray day feeling just a little warmer inside.

Because no matter how hard ballet got…

no matter how mean kids could be…

no matter how lonely home felt sometimes…

Brenda had done the first real thing that mattered.

She made a friend.

And for Brenda Holbul—

that was the beginning of everything.

CHAPTER FOUR

The next week moved like a slow parade.

Not slow like boring.

Slow like heavy.

Brenda Holbul started noticing things.

Not just ballet things.

Not just arm placement and foot angles and how Doris's eyes could slice through your soul like she had x-ray vision.

Brenda started noticing life things.

Like how some girls showed up with brand-new tights every class, bright and smooth like they came straight out of a package.

And some girls had tights that looked a little worn.

And some girls—like Brenda—had tights that Gloria washed carefully at night and hung up in the bathroom so they could dry without shrinking.

Gloria didn't complain out loud.

But Brenda could hear it anyway.

In the quiet.

In the way Gloria sighed when she sorted laundry.

In the way Gloria counted money on the kitchen table like the numbers were arguing back.

Brenda didn't understand bills.

But she understood pressure.

She understood when the air felt tight.

She understood when her mom smiled with her mouth but not with her eyes.

And she understood this too:

Ballet was expensive.

Ballet was the kind of dream that asked for money as an entry fee.

On Monday night, Gloria stood in the small kitchen holding a grocery receipt like it was a warning.

Brenda sat at the table drawing stick ballerinas with wide skirts and tiny crowns.

Gloria stared at the receipt again and then at Brenda's little dance bag sitting by the door.

The bag had Brenda's name written in black marker:

BRENDA

The marker had bled into the fabric a little. Not fancy. Not embroidered.

But it was hers.

Gloria finally spoke.

"Brenda, booboo," she said softly. "You like ballet?"

Brenda looked up fast.

"Yes."

Gloria nodded slowly like she was deciding something hard.

"You're sure?"

Brenda's face tightened with seriousness.

"I'm sure."

Gloria smiled and came over to the table.

She crouched and rested her cheek against Brenda's head for a second.

"Okay," Gloria whispered. "Then we're doing it."

Brenda didn't know what "we're doing it" meant the way a grown-up meant it.

Gloria meant: I will work myself to the bone to keep you in this class.

Brenda just heard: Yes.

And yes was everything.

Wednesday came again.

Brenda walked into the studio with her bag on her shoulder, hair pulled back tight, uniform clean.

She looked like a ballerina.

She didn't feel like one yet.

But she looked the part.

Inside, the room buzzed like always.

Little shoes squeaking.

Little voices echoing.

Mirror reflections multiplying everybody's movement like a spell.

Brenda saw Anastasia right away.

Anastasia waved both hands like Brenda was a celebrity.

Brenda smiled and waved back, dimples flashing.

She walked toward Anastasia and sat beside her again.

Anastasia leaned close.

"Hi Brenda," she said, like she was happy Brenda had returned safely from battle.

"Hi," Brenda whispered, still shy but less scared now.

Anastasia reached down and pulled at her tights, tugging them up like they were sliding down.

Brenda noticed Anastasia's tights were a little uneven.

A little twisted.

Brenda almost reached out to fix them like Doris did last week…

…but she didn't.

Brenda didn't want to act like a teacher.

She just sat quietly beside her friend.

Across the room, one of the Barbie girls was getting her hair adjusted by her mom.

Her mom hadn't left yet.

Some moms stayed for a minute longer.

Some moms hovered.

They had that look—like stage managers.

The Barbie girl's hair was slick and shiny,
sprayed tight like it could survive a hurricane.

Brenda watched for a second.

Then she looked away.

Doris always told them:

Leave the outside world outside.

But moms brought it in anyway.

Money. Perfection. Pressure.

All of it dragged into the studio like mud on expensive shoes.

Doris entered through the side door.

Clap.

"Line up."

The girls scrambled into their spots.

Brenda got into line faster than before, feeling proud she wasn't confused anymore.

She knew the rules now.

She knew what Doris wanted.

Or at least… she knew how to try.

Doris paced down the line.

She fixed a shoulder.

She corrected an elbow.

She adjusted a chin.

Then she stopped in front of one girl.

A small Latina girl with a serious face and bright eyes.

Her uniform straps were fine.

Her posture was fine.

But her hands were shaking.

Doris tilted her head slightly.

"What's wrong with you?" Doris asked.

Not mean.

Direct.

The Latina girl swallowed.

"I—I don't know."

Doris's eyes softened a fraction.

"You do know," Doris said quietly. "Say it."

The girl's face crumpled like paper.

Her mouth opened but nothing came out.

Her eyes started to fill.

Tears rose up fast like a flood behind a dam.

And then she made a sound…

A tiny choking sound.

And she started crying.

Not loud crying.

Not tantrum crying.

Real crying.

The kind that scares other kids because it feels too big for a small body.

The room went still.

Like someone had turned off the air.

Even the African American girls stopped talking.

Even the girls who always giggled went silent.

Brenda felt her stomach twist.

She didn't like seeing someone cry like that.

It felt like watching someone fall off a high place.

Doris didn't shout.

Doris didn't shame her.

Doris just crouched down, eye level with the girl.

"What is it?" Doris asked again, calm as stone.

The girl sniffled hard.

"My mom said if I'm not good… she's gonna stop bringing me."

Her voice came out broken.

The words hung in the air like smoke.

Brenda's eyes widened.

Stop bringing me.

Stop letting me dance.

Stop loving me the same?

That's what it sounded like.

The girl wiped her nose with the back of her hand and cried harder.

"She said I'm wasting money if I'm not good," the girl whispered.

And now the whole room felt different.

Because the girls didn't just hear the words.

They understood them.

Even at five years old, they understood that money mattered.

That being good mattered.

That love sometimes came with conditions.

Brenda stared at Doris.

Brenda waited to see what Doris would do.

Doris stood slowly.

She faced the whole class.

Her voice lowered into something serious.

"Listen to me," Doris said.

"You will all be good eventually."

Some girls blinked.

Some girls nodded without knowing why.

Doris continued.

"Not today. Not tomorrow. But you will be good if you show up. You will be good if you work."

Doris looked around the room.

"Some of you will be talented," she said. "And some of you will not."

That made a few girls stiffen.

Doris didn't care.

"But none of you," Doris said, louder now, "will act like talent is the only thing that matters."

She pointed toward the crying girl.

"She is here. That means she has heart."

The crying girl sniffled, tears still falling.

Doris's voice sharpened.

"A great man once said - Hustle beats talent, when talent don't hustle."

Doris continued

"And if your parents are foolish enough to think ballet is only worth it when you're perfect—"

Doris paused.

Her eyes flashed.

"—then those parents are wrong."

The room stayed silent.

Brenda's chest felt hot.

She didn't know why, but she felt like she wanted to cry too.

Not because she was sad for the girl.

Because Doris was saying things that sounded like truth.

Truth that grown-ups forget.

Doris turned back to the crying girl and softened again.

"Take a breath," Doris said.

The girl tried.

Doris said, "You belong here."

And that sentence hit the room like a spell.

You belong here.

Brenda swallowed hard.

Because Brenda wanted those words too.

Not from Doris.

From life.

From the world.

From her own bones.

After a few minutes, the girl calmed down.

Not fully.

But enough.

Doris clapped.

"First position."

The class started again.

The rhythm returned.

The work returned.

But something had changed.

The girls weren't just learning dance now.

They were learning pressure.

They were learning stakes.

They were learning that ballet wasn't all pink skirts and pretty poses.

Ballet was expectations.

Ballet was money.

Ballet was parents watching you like you were an investment.

And Brenda started realizing something deep in her five-year-old mind:

This place could make you strong.

Or it could break you.

Brenda practiced harder than she ever had.

She walked across the floor slow and steady.

She held her arms like she was holding something precious.

She kept her chin lifted even when her neck trembled.

She meant every movement.

Conviction.

Doris had said that word again in her head.

Brenda didn't forget it.

Brenda finished her turn and returned to the line.

She glanced at Anastasia.

Anastasia was clapping silently with her hands pressed together like she was proud.

Brenda smiled at her.

Dimples.

Anastasia smiled back, drool shining again, but still happy.

Still kind.

Still safe.

At the end of class, the girls packed up quietly.

The crying girl had stopped crying, but her eyes were red.

She looked embarrassed now.

Like she'd shown something ugly.

Brenda watched her carefully.

Brenda walked up to her.

Slow.

Shy.

She didn't know what to say, so she just said something small.

"It's okay," Brenda whispered.

The girl blinked at Brenda like she didn't expect kindness.

She nodded once.

Then she walked away fast, like she didn't want to cry again.

Brenda stood there for a second.

Then Anastasia waddled up next to Brenda.

Anastasia looked at Brenda's face.

"You good?" Anastasia asked.

Brenda smiled.

"Yeah," Brenda said. "I'm good."

Anastasia nodded like that settled it.

"Okay," she said, cheerful. "We stretch."

Brenda giggled softly.

"Yeah," Brenda agreed. "We stretch."

Outside, Gloria waited again in the van.

Brenda climbed in.

Gloria looked at her.

"Everything okay?" Gloria asked.

Brenda hesitated.

For one second, Brenda almost told her the truth.

That a girl cried because her mom might stop bringing her.

That ballet was scary sometimes.

That money sat in the room like a monster nobody wanted to name.

But Brenda didn't say all that.

Because Brenda didn't want Gloria to worry.

Brenda didn't want Gloria to see ballet as a problem.

Brenda wanted ballet to be a light.

So Brenda just said softly:

"Doris said we belong there."

Gloria's eyes flickered.

She swallowed hard.

She nodded like she was proud.

"You do belong there," Gloria said quietly. "Don't forget that."

Brenda leaned her head back against the seat.

The van rattled as it drove away.

And Brenda stared out the window, knowing now that ballet wasn't just dance.

It was a battlefield made of mirrors.

And she was learning how to survive it.

CHAPTER FIVE

Brenda Holbul woke up that morning with her stomach doing that thing again.

Not pain.

Not sickness.

Just nerves.

The kind that lived in your belly like a small animal pacing back and forth.

She laid in bed for a minute staring at the ceiling while her little brain ran through the same thoughts it always ran through before class.

Don't be weird.

Don't talk too loud.

Don't mess up.

Don't stand out.

Brenda had been living by those rules for so long, she didn't even realize they were rules.

They were just… survival.

Her mom, Gloria, had always told her to be polite. To be sweet. To be safe.

When you didn't have extra money, you didn't have extra mistakes either.

That's what life felt like.

No room for accidents.

Gloria braided Brenda's hair in the bathroom mirror before work.

Not fancy braids.

Not Instagram braids.

Just tight, clean, loving braids done by a tired mother with careful hands.

Gloria's fingers moved quick.

Brenda watched her mom's face in the mirror.

She saw the tiredness.

The calm strength.

The quiet determination.

Gloria wasn't the type to complain out loud.

But Brenda could still feel the weight of things in her home.

The bills.

The long work shifts at the library.

The way Gloria always made sure Brenda ate first.

The way Gloria always found a way to pay Doris, even when it meant buying cheaper groceries.

Gloria pulled the final elastic tight, then kissed Brenda's forehead.

"Okay," Gloria said. "You ready to go show 'em what you got?"

Brenda blinked.

She didn't hear that from Gloria often.

Not show 'em.

That sounded bold.

That sounded like Gloria believed in her more than Brenda believed in herself.

Brenda nodded slowly.

"Yeah," she whispered.

Then she took a breath.

And something strange happened.

Brenda thought:

Today… I'm going to talk.

Not because she was loud.

Not because she wanted attention.

But because she was tired of being scared.

And ballet, she was learning, wasn't just about dancing.

It was about courage.

The Astro Mini Van rumbled like always.

Gloria dropped Brenda at the curb, gave her one more kiss, and said the same soft thing she always said.

"Be good, booboo."

Brenda nodded.

But today, "be good" didn't mean "be invisible."

Today, it meant something else.

Today, it meant: be brave.

Brenda walked into the studio.

The warm wooden floors.

The huge mirrors.

The pastel walls.

The faint smell of perfume mixed with disinfectant.

And there they were.

The twelve girls.

Her world.

Her team.

Her competition.

Her sisters-in-training.

They were scattered around the room like butterflies.

Some stretching.

Some hopping.

Some laughing.

Some already in tiny social groups that looked sealed shut like clubs Brenda wasn't part of.

Brenda stood near the door for a moment, holding her bag close.

The old fear crawled up her throat.

But then she remembered something:

If you can face a mirror… you can face people too.

Brenda took a breath.

And walked forward.

A girl stood near the mirror adjusting her skirt.

She had long blonde hair, so smooth it looked like it had been combed by angels.

Her tights were perfect.

Her slippers looked brand new.

Her bag had sparkly letters stitched into it.

CLAIR THOMPSON

Even her name looked expensive.

Brenda swallowed.

This was the kind of girl that made Brenda feel small.

Not because she was mean.

Because she looked like she belonged in fancy places.

Like ballet was made for her.

Brenda stepped forward anyway.

She forced her voice out.

"Hi."

The blonde girl turned slowly.

Looked Brenda up and down.

Not rude.

Just curious.

"Hi," the girl replied.

Brenda felt her dimples appear when she smiled. It always happened when she was nervous.

"I'm Brenda," she said. "Brenda Holbul."

The blonde girl blinked once.

Then smiled like she decided Brenda was acceptable.

"I'm Clair Thompson," she said, like she was introducing herself to an audience.

Brenda nodded.

Clair's voice sounded confident. Like she'd never once asked herself if she belonged in a room.

Brenda wished she had that.

And then, out of nowhere, Clair asked—

"Do you like ballet?"

Brenda's whole face lit up.

"Yes," Brenda said quickly. "I'm trying really hard."

Clair laughed softly.

"I've been in dance since I was like… three."

Three.

Brenda felt her stomach dip.

She was already behind.

But she didn't let it show.

Instead she smiled and said—

"Wow. That's cool."

Clair shrugged like being impressive was normal for her.

But she didn't act cruel.

Not today.

Today she just looked… like a kid.

A kid with money and perfect hair, sure.

But still just a kid.

Clair leaned closer.

"I like when we do spins," Clair whispered. "Because then everyone has to watch."

Brenda giggled.

That was honest.

That was funny.

Brenda suddenly felt lighter.

Her fear loosened its grip.

And then she did something she'd never done before in this room.

She walked away from Clair… and didn't feel like she was running.

She felt like she was expanding.

Like she was turning into a social butterfly right in front of herself.

Brenda saw the three Latina girls gathered together, talking with their hands and laughing like their jokes had music in them.

One of them—the one Brenda had seen doing that little crip walk routine before—was bouncing lightly on her feet like she couldn't stop dancing even if she tried.

Brenda walked right up to them.

No hiding.

No hovering near the wall.

Brenda straightened her posture, took a breath, and said:

"Hi. I'm Brenda."

The three girls looked at her.

And Brenda—feeling bold now—pointed at the dancing girl and grinned.

"You got some moves there, ms.!"

The dancing girl's eyes widened.

Then she burst out laughing.

The other girls laughed too, and suddenly it didn't feel like Brenda was interrupting.

It felt like she had been invited.

The dancing girl tapped her chest.

"I'm Olga," she said proudly. "Olga Marquez."

Brenda nodded.

"Olga Marquez," Brenda repeated. "That's a cool name."

Olga smiled like she liked hearing it.

"I learned to dance from my cousin," Olga said. "Felipe. He's sixteen."

Brenda gasped like sixteen was ancient.

"Sixteen?" Brenda repeated. "That's like… a grown-up."

Olga laughed.

"Felipe thinks he's grown-up," Olga said. "He be dancing in the living room like he's famous."

The other Latina girls cracked up.

One of them said, "Felipe always tired though!"

Olga snapped her fingers like YES.

"Exactly!" Olga said. "He dance for five minutes and then he go sit down like an old man."

Brenda laughed so hard her dimples got deep.

She clutched her stomach.

"Dancing is hard," Brenda admitted, breathless.

Olga nodded like she respected that truth.

"Girl. Dancing is hard," Olga said seriously. "My legs be burning. I be like—why I do this to myself?"

Brenda giggled.

"Because it's fun," Brenda said.

Olga grinned.

"Because it's fun," Olga agreed.

And for a moment, right there—

it didn't feel like ballet.

It felt like childhood.

Then Anastasia walked up.

The bigger girl with the pigtails.

The one with the gentle drooling grin.

She waddled closer, smiling because she heard the laughter and wanted to be near it.

But the second the Latina girls saw her…

everything got quiet.

Not mean quiet.

Not cruel quiet.

Just the kind of quiet kids do when they don't know what to do.

They watched Anastasia.

Anastasia smiled wider.

A little drool slipped down her lip.

She didn't notice.

Brenda noticed though.

And Brenda felt her heart do something strong.

Like it clenched into a fist.

Not in anger.

In loyalty.

Brenda turned toward Anastasia and spoke immediately—clear, proud.

"This is my friend," Brenda said.

Then she smiled big and introduced her like she was announcing royalty.

"This is Anastasia."

Brenda looked at Anastasia too.

"Anastasia, this is Olga."

Olga blinked.

Then slowly smiled.

"Hi Anastasia," Olga said.

Anastasia lit up.

"Hi!" Anastasia said happily.

Brenda introduced the other Latina girls too, one by one, like she was making a bridge with her words.

And just like that—

the quiet broke.

The Latina girls started talking again.

Anastasia giggled.

Olga even laughed when Anastasia tried to copy a little foot move and almost fell over.

Brenda steadied her with a gentle hand.

Anastasia smiled at Brenda like Brenda was her hero.

And Brenda realized something deep:

Sometimes bravery isn't standing tall.

Sometimes bravery is making sure someone else isn't left out.

The laughter got bigger.

It spread.

It echoed off the mirrors.

And two heads turned across the room.

The African American girls heard it.

They saw the forming group.

The smiles.

The bouncing energy.

And they wanted in.

Because of course they did.

Joy pulls people toward it like gravity.

The two girls walked over, confident like they belonged anywhere they stepped.

One had big curls that bounced.

The other had braids with tiny beads clicking softly when she moved.

They stopped at the edge of the group like they were about to enter a party.

The curly-haired girl smiled first.

"Y'all laughing without us?" she asked playfully.

Olga's eyes widened.

Then she laughed.

"No!" Olga said. "Come here!"

The braided girl pointed at herself.

"I'm Kisha," she said proudly.

Then pointed to her friend.

"And that's Miyla."

Brenda smiled wide.

Dimples on full display.

"Hi, I'm Brenda," she said, voice steady. "This is Anastasia. And that's Olga."

The group laughed again.

Now everybody was talking at once.

Now the room felt warmer.

Now the air felt friendly.

Clair Thompson even wandered over like she'd been pulled in by the sound of fun.

Clair smiled cautiously, then relaxed when she saw everyone being nice.

And suddenly—

the studio didn't feel like a battlefield anymore.

It felt like a team.

Like a sisterhood.

Like a bunch of little girls who didn't have to be alone in their dreams.

They joked about dancing being hard.

They joked about their legs hurting.

They joked about how Doris looked like she could see through walls.

They laughed so much it felt like a real party.

And for a few magical minutes…

there was no jealousy.

No mean stares.

No silent measuring.

Just kids being kids.

Just laughter and love bouncing around the mirror room.

Then the side door opened.

Doris walked in.

Clipboard in hand.

Bun tight.

Eyes sharp.

She clapped once.

The whole room froze like she had pressed pause on life.

But Doris's face looked different today.

She wasn't irritated.

She wasn't annoyed.

She was…

smiling.

A small smile.

But real.

Doris looked at the girls, all grouped together, all bright-eyed and alive.

And Doris nodded like she approved.

"Good," Doris said calmly. "Good energy."

The girls settled into a line quickly, but they were still smiling.

Still glowing.

Doris paced in front of them.

"You girls are learning something important," Doris said.

She tapped the clipboard once.

"You are learning that ballet is discipline."

She paused.

"And ballet is sisterhood."

Brenda's chest warmed.

Because that word again.

Sisters.

Doris clapped again.

"Now," she said, voice firm but pleased, "we train."

The girls moved into first position.

Feet out.

Arms up.

Chins tall.

And today, for the first time…

Brenda wasn't just copying.

She wasn't just surviving.

She was part of something.

And when it came time for her to cross the floor…

she danced with conviction.

But now she also danced with joy.

Because she wasn't dancing alone anymore.

She had sisters.

CHAPTER SIX

The next week didn't feel like ballet anymore.

It felt like work.

Real work.

The kind that made your legs ache even when you were sitting still.

The kind that followed you home like a shadow and waited in your bedroom corner like a quiet bully.

Brenda Holbul used to think ballet was something you did in the studio.

Something special.

Something fancy.

Something that happened under mirrors and Doris's sharp eyes.

But now Brenda understood a new truth:

Ballet didn't start at the studio.
Ballet started at home.

On Monday evening, Gloria came home from the library with her shoulders slumped.

Her work shoes made that tired sound on the apartment floor—soft scuffs like she was dragging the day behind her.

Brenda was sitting on the living room carpet watching cartoons.

Her ballet slippers were beside her like they were waiting.

Gloria set her purse down slowly.

Then she looked at Brenda and smiled like she was trying to push the exhaustion out of her own face.

"Hey, booboo."

"Hi, Mom!"

Brenda bounced up and hugged her.

Gloria hugged back, tight.

Not the tightness of hair braids.

The tightness of love that was trying to hold everything together.

Gloria pulled away and touched Brenda's cheek.

"How was school?"

"Good," Brenda said.

Gloria nodded.

Then she glanced at Brenda's bag.

And Brenda knew what was coming.

Gloria didn't want to be the mean one.

But she had to be the responsible one.

"Okay," Gloria said softly. "Doris said ten minutes a day."

Brenda's stomach sank.

Ten minutes sounded small.

But it wasn't.

Ten minutes was forever when your muscles hurt.

Ten minutes was a long time to stand still and do everything right.

Brenda hesitated.

Gloria saw it immediately.

Her smile got thinner.

"Brenda…"

Brenda looked down at her slippers.

"I'm tired," she whispered.

Gloria exhaled slowly.

She didn't snap.

She didn't yell.

But her voice got firm—firm the way it got when Gloria had already decided the answer.

"I'm tired too," Gloria said quietly. "But we still do what we gotta do."

Brenda's eyes watered a little.

Because she didn't want to disappoint her mom.

And she didn't want to quit.

But she also wanted to be five years old.

She wanted to just… play.

Gloria crouched down so she was eye-level.

"You know why we practice at home?" Gloria asked.

Brenda sniffled. "So I can get good."

Gloria nodded.

"So you can get good," she repeated. "And so you don't have to feel scared in that room."

Brenda swallowed.

That hit hard.

Because it was true.

Brenda was scared in that room sometimes.

Even with friends now.

Even with Anastasia and Olga and Kisha and Miyla.

Even with Clair's fancy confidence shining in the corner.

Brenda still felt scared of being behind.

Gloria touched Brenda's shoulder.

"Come on," Gloria said softly. "Ten minutes."

Brenda stood up.

Slow.

Heavy.

Like she was walking toward punishment.

Gloria cleared a small space in the living room.

They didn't have a barre.

They didn't have a dance floor.

They didn't have mirrors along the wall.

They had carpet.

A coffee table.

A couch.

A lamp with a crooked shade.

And a mother who was trying her best.

Gloria put her hands on her hips.

"Okay," Gloria said, trying to sound cheerful. "First position."

Brenda turned her feet out.

Her knees wanted to collapse inward.

Her toes felt cramped in her slippers.

Her ankles felt wobbly.

"Arms," Gloria reminded.

Brenda lifted her arms like she was holding a beach ball.

Her shoulders rose immediately.

Gloria gently pushed them down.

"Relax," Gloria said. "No tension."

Brenda tried.

But her body didn't know how to relax while trying to be perfect.

Her brow furrowed.

She looked like she was solving a math problem.

Gloria smiled sadly.

"Why you looking like that?" Gloria asked.

Brenda's voice came out tiny.

"I wanna be good."

Gloria's eyes softened.

"I know," Gloria whispered. "I know, baby."

The first few days of practice were painful.

Not pain like injury.

Pain like growth.

Brenda's legs trembled in first position.

Her feet got sore faster than she thought they would.

Her arms got tired just holding them up.

It didn't make sense.

They weren't holding anything.

But ballet made your body hold itself like it was something precious.

That was the hardest part.

Brenda would finish practice and flop on the couch like a soldier done with training.

Sometimes she would whine.

Sometimes she would pout.

Sometimes she would say, "I don't wanna do ballet anymore."

And every time she said it, Gloria's face would flicker for half a second.

Like the words stabbed her.

Not because Gloria was mad.

Because Gloria heard something behind the words.

She heard: What if I can't keep paying?

She heard: What if my daughter gives up?

She heard: What if this dream was too expensive?

But Gloria never said any of that.

She just rubbed Brenda's head gently and said—

"Okay. You can feel that way."

Then she'd add:

"But you still gotta practice."

By Thursday, Brenda started to realize something else.

Practice wasn't just for ballet.

Practice was a war.

A quiet war inside your own mind.

A war between:

I want to quit

and

I want to win

Brenda didn't know what she wanted more.

Because quitting sounded like peace.

But winning sounded like pride.

Winning sounded like Doris nodding and saying "Good."

Winning sounded like her mom smiling without exhaustion hiding behind it.

So Brenda practiced.

Even when she didn't want to.

Even when her toes hurt.

Even when her legs burned.

Even when she wanted to throw her slippers out the window.

On Wednesday at the studio, Doris noticed the change.

Brenda walked in with her bag on her shoulder and her posture a little straighter.

She didn't look as nervous.

She didn't hover near the wall as long.

She went right to her friends.

Olga gave her a high-energy wave.

Kisha and Miyla were already laughing about something.

Clair looked perfect as always, but today she smiled at Brenda like they were equals.

And Anastasia waddled up and hugged Brenda without warning.

Brenda giggled and hugged her back.

"Okay," Doris said, clapping once. "Line up."

The girls got into place.

Doris's eyes swept over them.

Then she pointed her clipboard at them like a wand.

"Today," Doris said, "we see who practiced."

The girls stiffened.

Brenda's stomach flipped.

She practiced.

But did she practice enough?

Was it the right kind of practice?

Doris stepped to the front.

"First position."

The girls moved.

"Arms."

They lifted.

"Chins."

They raised.

Doris paced and corrected.

Then she stopped in front of Brenda.

Brenda held her breath.

Doris watched Brenda's feet.

Her knees.

Her arms.

Doris frowned slightly.

Brenda's heart dropped.

Then Doris said—

"Better."

Brenda blinked.

Doris said it again, louder this time.

"Better."

And the word hit Brenda's chest like a medal.

Brenda didn't smile big.

She didn't want to lose control.

But her dimples appeared anyway.

Doris stared at them for a second like she was amused.

Then Doris moved on.

But Brenda felt the warmth.

That warmth that said:

You're doing it.

That night, at home, Brenda practiced again.

Not because Gloria told her to.

Not because she was scared of Doris.

Because she wanted to.

Because she could feel it now.

She could feel the difference between last week's body and this week's body.

Her feet turned out easier.

Her arms held their shape longer.

Her posture didn't collapse so fast.

Brenda was becoming someone new.

Someone strong.

Someone disciplined.

Someone who did hard things even when nobody clapped.

Brenda practiced.

Then she walked into the kitchen where Gloria was standing over the sink doing dishes.

Gloria looked tired.

Her hair wasn't perfect.

Her work shirt was wrinkled.

But her hands still moved with care.

Brenda stepped up quietly.

"Mom?"

Gloria glanced over her shoulder.

"Yeah, booboo?"

Brenda's voice was soft.

"I practiced extra."

Gloria froze for a second.

Then she turned fully and looked at Brenda.

Her eyes watered just a little.

She tried to hide it.

But Brenda saw.

Gloria crouched down and kissed Brenda's forehead.

"I'm proud of you," Gloria whispered.

Brenda hugged her.

And in that hug, Brenda understood something she didn't have words for yet:

Gloria wasn't just paying for ballet lessons.

Gloria was paying for Brenda to become brave.

And Brenda wasn't just practicing for ballet.

Brenda was practicing for life.

CHAPTER SEVEN

By the time the next week rolled around, Brenda Holbul didn't feel like a visitor in her own body anymore.

She still wasn't the best.

She still wasn't the smoothest.

She still had moments where her feet felt confused and her arms got tired too fast and her brain panicked when Doris stared too long.

But something had changed.

Brenda wasn't just surviving ballet now.

She was building a version of herself that could handle it.

A tougher Brenda.

A braver Brenda.

A Brenda who practiced at home even when she wanted to flop on the couch and disappear into cartoons and snacks.

And the crazy part was…

Brenda started liking the hard part.

Because the hard part made her feel real.

On Tuesday night, Gloria came home late.

Later than usual.

Her keys jingled at the door and Brenda looked up from the floor where she was playing with little dolls.

Gloria's face looked worn-out in a way that Brenda didn't like.

Gloria smiled anyway, but her smile had fatigue behind it like a shadow.

"Hi, booboo," Gloria said, voice quiet.

Brenda stood up fast and hugged her.

Gloria hugged back tight.

Then she let out a breath like she'd been holding it all day.

"How was work?" Brenda asked.

Gloria didn't answer right away.

She walked into the kitchen, set her purse down, and stared at the counter like she forgot what she was supposed to do next.

Then she said softly:

"Busy."

Brenda watched her mom.

Sometimes kids can't understand grown-up problems…

but they can sense them.

Brenda sensed it.

Something was wrong.

Maybe not huge wrong.

But enough wrong to make the air feel heavy.

Gloria opened the fridge and pulled out leftovers.

She moved slow, like her body was begging to sit down.

Brenda stayed quiet for a second.

Then she spoke gently.

"Do you want me to practice now?"

Gloria turned and looked at her.

Her eyes widened just a little, like she couldn't believe Brenda said that without being asked.

Gloria swallowed.

Then she smiled—real this time.

"Yeah," Gloria said. "Let's do ten minutes."

Brenda nodded.

She went to get her slippers.

No complaining.

No pouting.

No war.

Not tonight.

Tonight Brenda practiced because she wanted to make Gloria feel proud.

Tonight Brenda practiced because she wanted Gloria to feel like all the work was worth it.

At the studio on Wednesday, the room felt different again.

Not hostile.

Not political.

Just… focused.

The girls joked and laughed before Doris arrived, but it wasn't chaos anymore.

It was friendship.

Olga bounced up to Brenda and said, "Girl, my legs still hurt from last week!"

Brenda giggled. "Mine too."

Kisha shook her head like she was offended by ballet itself.

"Why Doris want us suffering like this?" Kisha said dramatically.

Miyla laughed. "Because she evil."

Olga gasped and covered her mouth. "Shhh! Doris gon' hear you!"

The whole group laughed.

Even Clair smirked, elegant and quiet as always, like she didn't want to be seen laughing too hard.

Anastasia laughed the loudest, clapping her hands, drool shining on her lip like a tiny jewel again.

Brenda smiled at her.

Anastasia smiled back like she'd won a prize.

Brenda didn't feel alone anymore.

She felt like she had a squad.

Doris entered.

Clap.

"Line up."

The girls moved fast.

Doris's eyes scanned them as usual.

But her face didn't look annoyed.

Her face looked… interested.

Like she was measuring growth.

Not mistakes.

Doris walked to the front and held her clipboard against her side.

"Today," she said, "we do something new."

The room tightened.

New meant scary.

New meant you could fail in front of everybody.

Brenda felt her stomach flip.

Doris pointed toward the center of the floor.

"Today, each of you will do a short routine."

A few girls sucked in air.

One girl whispered, "Oh my God."

Olga elbowed her and whispered, "Girl, we five."

Kisha snorted.

Miyla giggled.

But Brenda didn't laugh.

Brenda's heart started pounding.

Routine meant…

everyone watches.

Everyone judges.

The mirror watches too.

Doris continued.

"Nothing big," she said. "Four steps. A pose. A turn. A bow."

She clapped once.

"You will do it one at a time."

The room went dead quiet.

Even Anastasia stopped moving.

Brenda stared at the floor.

Her palms felt sweaty.

Her throat felt dry.

She thought about quitting for a second.

Then she thought about Gloria.

The library.

The tired eyes.

The tight hugs.

The grocery receipts.

Brenda thought:

If Gloria can work all day… I can do four steps.

Brenda swallowed.

She stayed in line.

The first girl went.

Clair Thompson.

Of course Clair went first.

Clair walked out like she owned the studio floor.

Four steps—smooth.

Pose—perfect arms.

Turn—clean.

Bow—polished.

Clair didn't look nervous at all.

When she finished, some girls clapped softly.

Doris didn't clap.

Doris just nodded once, like a queen approving a performance.

"Good," Doris said.

Clair returned to line with her chin up.

Brenda watched her and felt two things at once.

Admiration.

And pressure.

Olga went next.

Olga's four steps had rhythm like music.

Her pose was playful.

Her turn was a little messy—but she recovered fast and bowed dramatically like she was a star.

Everyone laughed and clapped.

Even Doris's lips twitched like she was fighting a smile.

"Olga," Doris said, "this is ballet, not a street performance."

Olga grinned wide. "Sorry, Ms. Doris."

Doris shook her head.

"Again," Doris said, pointing. "More control."

Olga nodded, still smiling, and did it again. Cleaner this time.

Doris nodded.

"Better."

Kisha went.

Kisha didn't glide.

Kisha attacked the floor like she was making the floor respect her.

Her routine was strong.

Her pose was fierce.

Her turn was sharp.

Her bow looked like she was daring someone to criticize her.

Miyla clapped loud and yelled, "Period!"

The girls cracked up.

Doris raised one eyebrow.

"Kisha," Doris said dryly, "this is not a boxing match."

Kisha smiled sweetly like she hadn't just bullied the air into obedience.

"Yes ma'am."

Miyla went after.

Miyla was light.

She looked like a feather with sneakers on.

Even her mistakes looked cute.

She finished with a shy bow, and everyone clapped.

Doris nodded.

Then Anastasia.

Anastasia waddled out, smiling huge.

The room softened instantly.

Because Anastasia didn't make you nervous.

Anastasia made you feel human.

She took four steps slow.

Pose—arms drooping.

Turn—she nearly fell.

Then she caught herself, giggled, and bowed super low like she was bowing to a king.

The girls laughed.

Not cruel.

Warm.

Happy.

Doris walked over and gently lifted Anastasia's arms.

"Higher," Doris instructed.

Anastasia nodded.

"Okay," Anastasia said proudly.

Doris gave her a small smile.

"Good," Doris said.

Anastasia returned to line beaming like she'd won the Olympics.

Brenda's heart warmed.

Brenda's name came next.

Doris glanced at her clipboard.

"Brenda Holbul."

The room went quiet.

Brenda's stomach dropped into her shoes.

She stepped out into the center of the floor.

The mirrors swallowed her.

Twelve sets of eyes became twenty-four in the reflection.

Brenda felt tiny.

She felt exposed.

She felt like everybody could see every mistake she'd ever made.

Her arms trembled slightly.

Her feet felt too stiff.

She heard a voice inside her whisper:

Run back to the line.

But then another voice spoke up.

A stronger voice.

It sounded like Gloria.

It sounded like Doris.

It sounded like Brenda's future self.

It said:

No. Fix it.

Brenda inhaled slowly.

Her chin lifted.

Her shoulders dropped.

Her feet turned out.

Her arms rounded like holding a beach ball.

Brenda took four steps.

Slow.

Controlled.

Intentional.

Conviction.

She posed.

Her dimples didn't show.

Her face was serious.

Like she was taking an oath.

Then she turned.

It wasn't perfect.

But it was real.

And when she bowed…

she bowed like she meant it.

Like she wasn't asking for approval.

Like she was offering her heart.

The room stayed quiet.

For one long second.

Then Olga whispered loud enough for everyone to hear:

"Oooo okay Brenda!"

Kisha clapped twice.

Miyla clapped too.

Even Clair looked surprised.

Anastasia clapped the loudest, squealing, "Brendaaaa!"

Brenda felt her cheeks burn.

But inside her chest…

something rose up.

Not pride.

Not arrogance.

Something better.

Confidence.

Doris stared at Brenda for a moment.

Then she nodded slowly.

"Good," Doris said.

Then, as if that wasn't enough—

Doris added something she'd never added before.

"Brenda has presence."

Brenda's eyes widened slightly.

Presence again.

That word.

That powerful word.

Doris turned to the class.

"Some girls dance to look pretty," Doris said. "Some dance to copy. Some dance to be liked."

Doris's voice sharpened.

"Brenda dances like she means it."

Brenda swallowed hard.

She felt her throat tighten.

She fought the tears.

Not sad tears.

Overwhelmed tears.

Because being noticed felt good…

but it also felt dangerous.

Because being noticed meant expectations.

And expectations meant pressure.

But Brenda didn't run away from it.

She walked back to the line slowly.

Dignified.

And she stood beside her friends like she belonged.

When class ended, the girls gathered their bags.

The room felt warm.

Like they'd all survived something together.

Olga came up and grabbed Brenda's hand.

"Girl," Olga said, "you be dancing like you got a secret!"

Brenda laughed, dimples appearing.

"I don't!" Brenda insisted.

Kisha leaned in.

"You do," Kisha said. "I saw it. You be serious."

Miyla nodded. "Like you fighting the air."

Brenda giggled.

Anastasia waddled up and hugged Brenda again.

"You win," Anastasia said proudly.

Brenda hugged her back.

"I didn't win," Brenda whispered.

Anastasia shook her head like Brenda was silly.

"You win," Anastasia repeated.

And in Anastasia's simple world, maybe that was true.

Because winning didn't mean being the best.

Winning meant showing up.

Winning meant being brave.

Winning meant doing the routine instead of running away.

Outside, Gloria picked Brenda up after work.

Her mom looked tired again.

But when Brenda climbed into the passenger seat, she sat up straight, still holding that new confidence inside her like a warm secret.

Gloria glanced over.

"How was class?"

Brenda smiled.

Her dimples showed.

And her voice was soft but sure.

"I did a solo."

Gloria froze for a second.

"A solo?" she repeated.

Brenda nodded proudly.

"Yeah. Doris said I have… presence."

Gloria's eyes watered instantly.

She blinked fast, trying not to cry in the driver's seat.

Her voice came out quiet.

"That's… that's amazing, baby."

Brenda nodded, staring out the window as the van drove away.

And for the first time, Brenda didn't just feel like a little girl learning ballet.

She felt like someone becoming something.

Someone building herself.

Step by step.

Pose by pose.

Breath by breath.

CHAPTER NINE

After the "money thing," the studio didn't feel the same anymore.

It still smelled like wooden floors and hair spray and clean mirrors…

…but Brenda Holbul felt like there was something invisible in the air now.

Something that wasn't there before.

A crack.

A dent.

A reminder.

It wasn't loud.

Nobody was screaming or fighting.

But it was there.

In the way girls looked at Brenda just a second too long.

In the way some of them stopped smiling when she walked by.

In the way laughter could go quiet fast if Doris wasn't in the room yet.

Brenda didn't want to be scared.

She didn't want to be bitter.

She didn't want to feel like she didn't belong.

But part of her did.

And once that feeling gets in your chest…

it sits there like a stone.

At home, Gloria tried not to talk about it.

Gloria didn't bring up "poor."

She didn't bring up conditioner.

She didn't bring up Clair Thompson or anybody else.

She just cooked dinner, cleaned up, and acted like life was normal.

But Brenda could tell her mom was protecting her.

Like Gloria was holding her anger under the surface so it wouldn't spill on Brenda.

One night, after Brenda finished practice, she sat on the couch and stared at her slippers.

They looked soft and worn.

Used.

Loved.

Not fancy.

Brenda ran her fingers along the edge of one slipper and whispered:

"Mom…"

Gloria was at the sink doing dishes.

"Yeah, booboo?"

Brenda hesitated.

Then her voice came out small.

"Am I… embarrassing?"

The dishwater stopped running.

Gloria turned around slowly.

Her face didn't look angry.

It looked hurt.

Gloria walked over and crouched in front of Brenda like she was talking to someone important.

Because she was.

"Brenda," Gloria said firmly, "you are not embarrassing."

Brenda's eyes watered.

Gloria touched Brenda's cheek.

"People who pick on you," Gloria continued, "they're the embarrassing ones."

Brenda sniffled.

"But they laughed," Brenda whispered.

Gloria's expression changed.

It got sharper.

Stronger.

"Then let them laugh," Gloria said. "You don't answer laughing with crying."

Brenda blinked.

Gloria leaned closer.

"You answer with excellence."

That word felt big.

Excellence.

It didn't sound like a kid word.

It sounded like a warrior word.

Brenda swallowed hard and nodded.

"Okay," she whispered.

Gloria kissed her forehead.

"That's my baby," Gloria said softly.

Wednesday came again.

Ballet day.

Brenda stared at herself in the bathroom mirror while Gloria fixed her hair.

The hair wasn't perfect.

Still no conditioner.

Still a few flyaways.

Still little stubborn pieces that refused to obey.

Gloria did her best.

And Brenda decided she would do hers too.

But before they left, Gloria pulled something out of her purse.

A small, cheap pack of hair ties.

Not the fancy kind.

Just plain.

But new.

Gloria handed them to Brenda.

Brenda stared at them.

Gloria spoke softly.

"I found these on sale."

Brenda's throat tightened.

She didn't say thank you right away.

Because thank you wasn't enough.

Brenda hugged her mom hard.

Gloria hugged back.

Then Gloria cleared her throat like she was trying not to cry.

"Come on," Gloria whispered. "Let's go."

At the studio, Brenda walked in feeling like she was walking into a test.

Not a ballet test.

A life test.

The room buzzed with small chatter.

Olga waved at Brenda instantly.

Kisha and Miyla were talking quieter than usual.

Anastasia stood near the wall, smiling like she was waiting for Brenda like always.

Clair Thompson stood near the mirror again, perfect as ever.

Brenda felt her stomach tighten when she saw her.

Clair looked at Brenda too.

Their eyes met.

Clair didn't smile.

But she didn't insult Brenda either.

She just looked away.

That almost felt worse.

Because it felt like Brenda was something she didn't want to look at.

Like poverty was contagious.

Brenda took a breath.

And walked forward anyway.

She wasn't going to shrink.

Not today.

Not ever.

Doris entered.

Clap.

"Line up."

The girls lined up fast.

Doris's eyes scanned them like always.

But today she didn't start with first position.

Today she held her clipboard close and spoke first.

Her voice was calm, but there was iron under it.

"Before we begin," Doris said, "I want something understood."

The room went still.

Even the girls who usually giggled stopped.

Doris paced once in front of the line.

"In ballet," Doris said, "every one of you will face pain."

The girls stared.

Doris continued.

"Your legs will hurt. Your toes will hurt. Your pride will hurt."

That hit them.

Because kids understood pride even if they didn't understand taxes.

Doris looked down the line.

"And some of you," Doris said, "will try to ease your pain by putting it on someone else."

The room got colder.

Brenda felt her throat tighten.

Doris's gaze swept over the girls.

It didn't land on anyone too long.

But it didn't have to.

Everyone knew what she meant.

Then Doris said something that made the whole studio feel like it shifted.

"Not in my room."

Her voice didn't rise.

It didn't need to.

It had weight.

"Not in my room," Doris repeated. "Not in my studio. Not in my presence."

Some girls looked down.

Some swallowed hard.

Clair's face stayed stiff.

Doris nodded once, like she'd hammered a nail into place.

"Good," Doris said. "Now we work."

The class started.

First position.

Arms.

Chins.

Across the floor.

The usual.

But Brenda felt different.

She wasn't dancing to be liked.

She wasn't dancing to prove she wasn't poor.

She wasn't dancing to win some invisible popularity contest.

Brenda was dancing for herself.

For Gloria.

For the version of Brenda that might be older one day… and proud.

Brenda stepped across the floor.

Slow.

Controlled.

Conviction.

She posed with intention.

She turned with care.

And even though her turn wasn't perfect—

she didn't panic.

She didn't collapse.

She recovered.

And Doris noticed.

Doris always noticed.

Doris walked past Brenda and said quietly, so quiet only Brenda could hear:

"That's how you come back."

Brenda's heart jumped.

Come back.

That meant Doris saw what happened last week.

It meant Doris knew Brenda was fighting a battle inside herself.

And it meant Doris was proud of her for not giving up.

Brenda didn't smile.

She stayed serious.

But a dimple tried to appear anyway.

Brenda held it back.

Not because she wasn't happy.

But because she didn't want the other girls to think she was showing off.

Because she still feared their jealousy.

And that fear was real now.

During stretching, Olga scooted closer to Brenda and whispered:

"You okay today?"

Brenda nodded.

Olga's face softened.

"I wanted to say something last week," Olga whispered. "But I got scared."

Brenda looked at Olga.

Olga's eyes were wide.

Guilty.

Honest.

Brenda understood that too.

Fear made people freeze.

Fear made you quiet when you should be loud.

Brenda whispered back, "It's okay."

Olga exhaled like she'd been holding her breath for days.

Then Olga smiled.

And for the first time all day…

Brenda smiled too.

Dimples.

Just a little.

Kisha and Miyla approached after class.

Kisha looked like she didn't want to be there.

Like apologizing tasted bad.

But Miyla nudged her.

"Kisha," Miyla whispered.

Kisha rolled her eyes.

Then she sighed.

"Brenda," Kisha said bluntly.

Brenda looked at her.

Kisha's voice softened just a fraction.

"My bad."

Brenda blinked.

Kisha looked away quickly like she hated being vulnerable.

Miyla stepped forward next.

"I'm sorry too," Miyla said. "We shouldn't have laughed."

Brenda nodded slowly.

Her voice came out small but steady.

"Thank you."

Kisha shrugged.

Then muttered, "You still got that serious dancing face though."

Brenda giggled.

Miyla laughed too.

Olga laughed from behind them.

And for a second… the tension cracked.

Not gone.

But cracked enough for light to leak through.

Anastasia waddled up and wrapped her arms around all of them like she was hugging a pile of laundry.

"Friends!" Anastasia yelled happily.

The girls laughed.

Even Kisha.

Even Clair, watching from across the room, looked like she almost smiled before stopping herself.

When Brenda got into the van, Gloria looked over immediately.

"How was it?"

Brenda buckled herself in and stared forward.

She thought about the day.

Doris's speech.

The quiet apology.

The way her body felt stronger.

The way she didn't collapse under shame.

Brenda took a breath.

Then she said quietly:

"I came back."

Gloria's eyes softened.

She nodded.

"That's my baby," Gloria whispered. "That's my strong girl."

The van drove away.

And Brenda leaned her head against the window, watching the studio shrink behind her.

She didn't feel victorious.

Not yet.

But she felt steady.

She felt like she was learning how to take hits.

How to stand back up.

How to keep dancing even when the world got mean.

And that…

was the quiet comeback.

CHAPTER ELEVEN

After Doris said the word recital, everything in ballet became sharper.

The room didn't change.

The mirrors didn't move.

The floors were still the same warm wood.

But the energy changed.

Like everybody suddenly realized they weren't just playing ballerina anymore.

They were becoming ballerinas.

And becoming something serious came with pressure.

Pressure came with mistakes.

And mistakes came with fear.

Brenda Holbul felt it in her bones.

At home, Gloria started setting a timer.

Not in a harsh way.

Not like punishment.

Just… like routine.

Like something they did because that's what serious people did.

"Ten minutes," Gloria would say.

Then she'd glance at Brenda and add:

"Okay… fifteen."

Brenda didn't fight anymore.

Not like before.

Sometimes her legs still hurt. Sometimes she wanted to quit.

But she'd learned that wanting to quit didn't mean she would quit.

It just meant her body was tired.

It meant she was growing.

So Brenda practiced.

She practiced in the living room on carpet that grabbed her slippers and made turning harder.

She practiced near the couch, careful not to kick the coffee table.

She practiced with Gloria watching like a tired coach who loved her athlete too much to ever give up.

And every time Brenda nailed a move—just one clean turn, one clean pose—Gloria would smile like it paid off all the bills.

That smile made Brenda push harder.

At the studio the following Wednesday, Doris didn't waste time.

No warm-up laughter.

No long chatter.

She clapped the moment she walked in.

Clap.

"Line up."

The girls scrambled into place fast.

Even Olga was quiet.

Even Kisha stopped joking.

Even Clair looked focused instead of perfect.

Doris's eyes scanned them like she was about to choose warriors for battle.

"Recital routine," Doris said. "Now."

The girls moved into position.

Brenda's heart started thumping faster.

The routine wasn't hard.

But it had to be together.

It had to be smooth.

It had to look like one body made of twelve little girls.

Doris stood off to the side, clipboard tucked against her ribs like a weapon.

"From the top," Doris commanded.

And they began.

Four steps forward.

Pose.

Arms up.

Turn.

Two steps back.

Bow.

Repeat.

They ran it once.

Then again.

Then again.

And the more they practiced it, the more Doris tightened the screws.

"Cleaner!" Doris snapped.

"Control!"

"No sloppy arms!"

"Chin up!"

Brenda did her best.

She tried so hard her face looked stiff.

Her dimples disappeared completely.

It wasn't fear anymore.

It was concentration.

It was hunger.

It was the need to not fail.

During a short water break, the girls sat on the floor.

Olga fanned herself with her hands.

"Doris trying to kill us," Olga whispered.

Kisha nodded. "I'm about to file a complaint."

Miyla giggled. "To who?"

Clair sipped her water with her pinky slightly lifted, like she couldn't help herself.

"We'll survive," Clair said.

Kisha stared at her.

"Clair, you talk like a princess," Kisha said.

Clair shrugged. "My mom says I have good diction."

Olga burst out laughing.

Brenda smiled too, but her stomach still felt twisted.

Something in her felt off.

Her legs were tired today.

More tired than usual.

Maybe she practiced too hard the night before.

Maybe she didn't eat enough breakfast.

Maybe her body was just having one of those days where it didn't feel like obeying.

Brenda glanced at Gloria's old watch on her wrist—Gloria let her wear it sometimes because it made Brenda feel grown.

The watch was too big, sliding around her arm.

Brenda liked the weight of it.

It felt like responsibility.

But responsibility was heavy.

And Brenda was small.

Doris clapped.

"Back up. Again."

The girls stood.

Brenda stood too, taking a breath.

She rolled her shoulders once, trying to relax the tension out.

Doris pointed to the line.

"Brenda," Doris said suddenly. "Front."

Brenda froze.

Front?

Her stomach dropped.

Doris pointed again.

"Front center. You lead this time."

The girls looked at Brenda.

Brenda felt her face heat.

She didn't want to lead.

Leading meant eyes on you.

Leading meant blame if anything went wrong.

Leading meant pressure so thick you could chew it.

Brenda's lips parted.

She almost whispered "I can't."

But then she remembered Gloria's words.

Answer with excellence.

Brenda swallowed hard.

And stepped forward.

Front center.

The mirror showed her doubled.

Twelve girls behind her like backup dancers.

Brenda's heart hammered.

Doris's voice cut through the room.

"From the top," Doris said.

Brenda raised her arms.

The girls followed.

Brenda stepped forward.

One.

Two.

Three.

Four.

Pose.

So far so good.

Brenda turned.

Her foot slipped.

Not a big slip.

A tiny slip.

But tiny slips became disasters in ballet.

Brenda's ankle wobbled.

Her balance snapped.

And the next thing she knew—

Brenda's body dropped sideways like a doll.

She fell.

Hard.

Slap of skin on wood.

A sound louder than it should've been.

The room froze.

Everything stopped.

Brenda's breath vanished.

Pain hit her hip.

Not sharp enough to break.

Sharp enough to humiliate.

Brenda's eyes filled instantly.

Her cheeks burned hotter than the pain.

She stared at the ceiling.

For one second she couldn't move.

Like her body needed permission.

She heard someone gasp.

She heard a small laugh try to escape someone's mouth and get swallowed back down.

She heard Olga whisper, "Oh no…"

And then she heard Doris's shoes crossing the floor.

Quick steps.

Firm steps.

Doris crouched beside Brenda.

Her voice came out calm.

"Are you injured?"

Brenda shook her head fast even though she didn't know for sure.

"No," Brenda whispered.

Her voice cracked.

Doris nodded once.

"Good," Doris said.

Brenda blinked through tears.

Doris leaned in closer.

"Now get up."

The words were sharp.

Not mean.

Exact.

Brenda trembled as she pushed herself up off the floor.

Her hip hurt.

Her pride hurt worse.

She stood there, arms still lifted, face red, tears spilling down like she couldn't stop them.

She hated the tears.

She hated how weak they made her feel.

She hated the attention.

She hated that she'd fallen in front of everyone.

Brenda sniffled hard.

She tried to wipe her face with her wrist.

Doris's hand gently caught her arm.

"No," Doris said quietly.

Brenda froze.

Doris looked into Brenda's eyes.

"You don't hide it," Doris said. "You don't run."

Brenda's lips trembled.

Doris's voice lowered into something fierce.

"You fall like a dancer," Doris said. "And you rise like one too."

Brenda swallowed.

Doris pointed to the line again.

"Again," Doris commanded.

Brenda stared.

Again?

With tears still on her face?

With her hip aching?

With her heart cracked open?

Doris's expression didn't change.

"Again," Doris repeated.

The room waited.

Twelve little girls watching.

The mirrors watching too.

Brenda took a shaking breath.

Then she nodded.

She turned back to position.

Front center.

Still crying.

Still embarrassed.

Still scared.

But standing.

Brenda lifted her arms again.

Not perfect arms.

But determined arms.

Doris clapped.

"From the top."

Brenda stepped forward.

One.

Two.

Three.

Four.

Pose.

Turn.

This time she stuck it.

She held the balance.

She recovered.

She moved through the rest of the routine on pure willpower.

Her face stayed wet.

Her dimples stayed hidden.

But her conviction showed through anyway.

When she bowed, it wasn't pretty.

It was brave.

When she finished, there was silence.

Then Doris nodded.

"Good," Doris said.

And that word didn't feel small today.

It felt enormous.

After class, the girls packed up quietly.

Brenda moved slow.

Her hip ached.

She didn't want anyone to see her limp.

Olga walked up first.

Olga didn't joke.

Olga didn't bounce.

Olga just looked at Brenda like she meant it.

"You okay?" Olga asked softly.

Brenda nodded.

Kisha and Miyla came next.

Miyla looked worried.

Kisha looked uncomfortable.

Like she didn't know how to be gentle.

But even Kisha spoke quietly.

"That was… kinda hard," Kisha muttered. "But you got back up."

Brenda nodded again.

Anastasia hugged Brenda hard like she was trying to squeeze the pain out of her body.

"You strong," Anastasia whispered.

Brenda hugged back.

And for a second, the sting of the fall didn't feel so heavy.

Outside, Gloria pulled up.

The van door opened.

Brenda climbed in slowly.

Gloria took one look at her daughter's face and knew.

"Brenda…" Gloria said, worried. "What happened?"

Brenda stared out the window, fighting tears again.

Her voice came out small.

"I fell."

Gloria's hands tightened on the steering wheel.

Then she reached over and touched Brenda's knee gently.

"Did it hurt?"

Brenda nodded.

"My hip," she whispered.

Gloria's face tightened like she wanted to cry and yell at the same time.

But she didn't.

She breathed slowly.

Then she asked the most important question.

"Did you get back up?"

Brenda paused.

She remembered Doris's voice.

Now get up.

She remembered the moment her legs shook but still moved.

Brenda nodded slowly.

"Yes," she said.

Gloria's expression softened like sunlight breaking through clouds.

She kissed Brenda's forehead.

"That's my girl," Gloria whispered.

Brenda leaned her head against the window, watching the studio disappear behind them.

The fall had hurt.

It had humiliated her.

It had made her cry.

But it had also taught her something important.

She wasn't just a ballerina when she was perfect.

She was a ballerina when she was broken…

…and still chose to stand.

CHAPTER TWELVE

The bruise on Brenda Holbul's hip turned purple the next day.

Not a cute little bruise either.

A real bruise.

The kind that made her walk carefully.

The kind that made sitting down feel like landing wrong all over again.

Gloria noticed it the moment Brenda shuffled into the kitchen that morning.

Gloria's eyes narrowed.

"Let me see," she said.

Brenda lifted her pajama shirt a little so Gloria could look.

Gloria sucked in a breath.

"Sweet baby Jesus…" Gloria whispered.

Brenda blinked.

Gloria wasn't even the type to say stuff like that.

Which meant the bruise was bad.

Brenda tried to laugh like it didn't matter.

"It's okay, Mom," Brenda said quickly. "It doesn't really hurt."

Gloria gave her a look.

A mom look.

The look that said you can lie to yourself, but you can't lie to me.

Gloria knelt down to Brenda's height and kissed her forehead.

"You're tough," Gloria said softly. "But tough girls still get rest."

Brenda nodded slowly.

Gloria stood back up.

"And you're still going to ballet," Gloria added.

Brenda's stomach flipped.

Even with the bruise?

Gloria's face stayed firm.

"Yeah," Gloria said. "Because you don't quit because of bruises. You quit when you stop loving it."

Brenda swallowed.

Then she nodded.

Because she still loved it.

Even when it hurt.

Especially when it hurt.

At school that day, Brenda felt different.

Not just sore.

Different inside.

She kept thinking about the fall.

The sound of her body hitting the floor.

The way the room froze.

The way she wanted to disappear so badly she could taste it.

And she kept thinking about Doris's voice.

You fall like a dancer. And you rise like one too.

Brenda didn't fully understand that sentence…

but she felt it.

She felt like she'd crossed some invisible line.

Like she wasn't just "a little girl in ballet class" anymore.

She was becoming one of those kids who could take a hit.

A kid with grit.

Wednesday arrived again.

And Brenda almost didn't want to go.

Not because she was scared of Doris.

Not because she hated ballet.

But because she didn't want to walk back into that room where she fell.

Brenda didn't want to face the mirrors.

They would show her the bruise if she turned sideways.

They would show her body like it remembered the impact.

Brenda didn't want to face the other girls either.

Not because they were mean.

Because she didn't want to be remembered as the girl who fell.

Brenda sat in the van quietly on the drive over.

Gloria noticed.

"You nervous?" Gloria asked gently.

Brenda nodded.

Gloria exhaled.

Then she spoke low, like she was giving Brenda a spell.

"Brenda… falling doesn't ruin you."

Brenda stared at her mom.

Gloria's eyes were tired, but steady.

"Staying down ruins you," Gloria finished.

Brenda nodded slowly.

The van pulled up.

And Brenda stepped out.

Bruised hip and all.

Inside the studio, the girls were already there.

The mirrors were the same.

The floors were the same.

The air was the same.

But Brenda's heart was pounding like the room might swallow her.

She stepped in quietly.

Instantly, Olga saw her.

Olga's eyes widened like she'd been waiting.

"Brenda!" Olga called out.

Brenda flinched.

Her first thought was:

Oh no. Everyone's gonna look.

And they did.

But not in a cruel way.

In a concerned way.

Olga jogged over and grabbed Brenda's hand gently.

"Girl! Are you okay?" Olga asked.

Brenda blinked.

She didn't expect that.

Brenda nodded.

"My hip is kinda… hurt," Brenda admitted.

Olga's face twisted like she was angry at the floor for attacking her friend.

"That floor mean," Olga muttered.

Brenda giggled a little.

Then Kisha and Miyla walked up too.

Miyla's voice was soft.

"Does it still hurt?"

Brenda nodded again.

Kisha leaned closer like she was inspecting damage.

"Lemme see," Kisha said.

Brenda hesitated.

But she lifted her shirt slightly again.

Kisha's eyes got big.

"OH!" Kisha said loudly. "Girl, you got hit-hit!"

Miyla covered her mouth.

Olga gasped dramatically.

Anastasia waddled up through the group, smiling, then stopped when she saw everyone staring.

"What?" Anastasia asked, worried.

Brenda pointed to her hip area.

"I fell," Brenda said simply.

Anastasia's face fell.

Then she hugged Brenda so fast and hard it nearly knocked Brenda over again.

"NO FALL," Anastasia protested, like she was arguing with reality itself.

Brenda laughed even though it hurt her hip a little.

"That's what I said," Brenda whispered.

And in that moment…

the shame loosened.

Just a little.

Because nobody was laughing at her fall.

Nobody was calling her clumsy.

Nobody was making it her identity.

They were just… caring.

Like real friends.

Like sisters.

Clair Thompson approached last.

She moved slower than the others.

More careful.

Like she wasn't sure she was allowed in the circle.

Clair's eyes landed on Brenda's face.

Then her hip.

Then her bag.

Clair's expression shifted.

Not to pity.

To something like respect.

Clair spoke quietly.

"Are you okay?"

Brenda blinked.

Clair asking that felt… big.

Brenda nodded.

"I'm okay," Brenda said.

Clair hesitated, then added:

"That was… brave. When you got back up."

Brenda's throat tightened.

She didn't know how to respond to kindness from Clair.

Clair used to feel like pressure in a human form.

Now she just looked like a kid who didn't know how to fix the bad things she helped start.

Brenda gave her a small smile.

Dimples appeared.

"Thank you," Brenda whispered.

Clair nodded once.

Then she stood with the group.

And just like that…

the circle was complete again.

Doris entered through the side door.

Clap.

The room snapped into order fast.

But Doris paused for half a second when she saw the girls grouped up.

Doris didn't look annoyed.

She looked… pleased.

Not that she'd admit it out loud.

The girls lined up.

Doris stepped forward.

"Brenda," Doris said calmly.

Brenda's stomach flipped again.

Doris glanced at her posture.

At her stance.

At the careful way Brenda held herself.

"You injured?" Doris asked.

Brenda swallowed.

"Not really," Brenda said.

Doris raised one eyebrow.

That look again.

The one that said be honest in my room.

Brenda corrected herself.

"My hip is bruised."

Doris nodded once.

"Okay," Doris said. "No big leaps today."

Brenda exhaled in relief.

Then Doris said something unexpected.

"But you will still work."

Brenda nodded.

"Good," Doris said.

Doris faced the class.

"Ladies," Doris announced, "this is how dancers are made."

She pointed to Brenda without making a big show of it.

"Not when everything goes right," Doris said. "When things go wrong."

The girls listened.

Even the gigglers.

Even Olga.

Even Kisha.

Doris continued.

"A dancer falls. A dancer hurts. A dancer is embarrassed."

Brenda's face warmed again, but this time it wasn't shame.

It was understanding.

Doris's voice got lower.

"And a dancer returns."

Brenda's heart clenched.

Doris clapped once.

"Now. Recital routine."

They practiced again.

This time Brenda didn't lead.

Doris positioned her safely toward the middle.

Brenda still gave conviction.

Still meant every movement.

But now she watched the other girls too.

She watched Olga trying to control her energy.

She watched Kisha learning to be smooth instead of strong.

She watched Miyla trying to stop rushing ahead.

She watched Clair trying not to look annoyed.

She watched Anastasia fighting to keep her arms up, even when they got tired.

And Brenda realized something.

They were all struggling.

Not just her.

They all had battles.

Some battles were inside their bodies.

Some were inside their families.

Some were inside their pride.

But everybody was fighting something.

And that made Brenda feel less alone.

During stretches, the girls sat together.

Kisha leaned toward Brenda and whispered:

"You know what I learned?"

Brenda looked at her.

Kisha smirked.

"I learned I would cry if I fell like that."

Miyla giggled.

Olga nodded seriously.

"I would've screamed," Olga said. "Like full scream."

Anastasia whispered loudly, "I would bite the floor."

The girls burst out laughing.

Brenda laughed too—so hard it made her hip ache, but she didn't care.

Because that laugh felt like medicine.

That laugh felt like glue.

It stitched up the little tear that shame had made inside her.

And Brenda realized something else.

Friendship wasn't just giggling when life was good.

Friendship was the group standing around your bruise and saying:

We're still here.

When class ended, the girls didn't rush out like usual.

They lingered.

They packed slow.

Olga took Brenda's hand again.

"Come on," Olga said. "We walk out together."

Brenda blinked.

"Okay," Brenda whispered.

Clair fell into step beside them.

Kisha and Miyla followed.

Anastasia waddled behind, humming happily like she didn't know any of the world's darkness.

They walked out as a group.

Twelve tiny ballerinas moving like one big sisterhood.

Not perfect.

But together.

In the van, Gloria looked at Brenda immediately.

"How was it today?" Gloria asked.

Brenda leaned back and took a breath.

Then she smiled.

Dimples and all.

"It was good," Brenda said.

Gloria's eyes softened.

"Good how?"

Brenda stared out the window and chose her words carefully.

"Like… everybody fixed it," Brenda whispered.

Gloria frowned slightly. "Fixed what?"

Brenda looked back at her mom.

"The fall," Brenda said simply.

Gloria's eyes watered again.

She nodded like she understood.

"Good," Gloria whispered.

Then she added, voice full of pride:

"That's how family works."

Brenda leaned her head against the window.

The bruise still hurt.

But it didn't feel like shame anymore.

It felt like proof.

Proof that she fell…

and didn't break.

And proof that she had sisters around her…

who wouldn't let her.

CHAPTER THIRTEEN

By the time the recital got close, everything in Brenda Holbul's life started feeling like it had rhythm.

Not just ballet rhythm.

Life rhythm.

Wake up.

School.

Homework.

Dinner.

Practice.

Sleep.

Repeat.

It was the kind of routine that made Brenda feel like a real ballerina.

Like she wasn't playing dress-up anymore.

Like she was becoming something.

But it also made the house quieter.

Because routines didn't leave space for extra.

Extra money.

Extra time.

Extra energy.

Gloria Holbul was running on fumes.

And Brenda could tell.

Not because Gloria complained.

Gloria almost never complained.

But Brenda heard it in the silence.

In the pauses between words.

In the way Gloria sometimes stared at the wall for a second too long before moving again.

In the way she rubbed her temples like she was pressing stress back into her skull.

Brenda watched all of it with the quiet understanding only kids can have.

Kids couldn't fix grown-up problems.

But they could feel them.

And it hurt.

On Tuesday night, the sky outside was dark and rainy.

The kind of rain that didn't sound peaceful.

The kind that sounded restless.

Brenda practiced in the living room while Gloria sat on the couch with her shoes still on, exhaustion sitting on her shoulders like a heavy coat.

Gloria had her library lanyard still around her neck.

She hadn't even taken it off yet.

Brenda stood in first position.

Feet turned out.

Arms rounded.

Chin up.

She took four steps forward and froze in a pose like Doris taught her.

Gloria watched quietly.

Not with a smile.

Not with criticism.

Just… watching.

Brenda did the routine again.

Then again.

Brenda's legs began to tremble.

Her hip still felt tender from the bruise.

She tried not to show it.

But Gloria saw everything.

Gloria always saw everything.

Brenda took another step.

Her ankle wobbled.

She caught herself.

Then she let out a frustrated breath and lowered her arms.

"I'm tired," Brenda whispered.

Gloria nodded slowly.

"I know."

Brenda stared at the carpet.

Her voice got smaller.

"Are you tired too?"

Gloria laughed once.

Not a happy laugh.

A tired laugh.

"A little," Gloria admitted.

Brenda's throat tightened.

Brenda didn't want Gloria tired.

Brenda didn't want Gloria stressed.

Brenda didn't want ballet to be something that drained her mother.

Brenda wanted ballet to be something that gave back.

Something joyful.

Something magical.

But sometimes magic cost money.

And money was something their house didn't have extra of.

Brenda swallowed.

Then she whispered the thing she didn't want to say.

"Mom… if it's too much… I can stop."

Gloria froze.

Like the air got pulled out of the room.

She slowly sat up straighter.

Her eyes locked on Brenda.

Brenda's stomach dropped.

She thought maybe she'd made Gloria angry.

But Gloria wasn't angry.

Gloria looked like she'd been punched in the chest.

"Don't say that," Gloria whispered.

Brenda blinked.

Gloria stood up and walked toward Brenda slowly.

Her voice was soft, but intense.

"Brenda," Gloria said, kneeling down, "you don't quit something you love because I'm struggling."

Brenda's eyes filled.

"But you work so much," Brenda said. "And we don't have—"

Brenda stopped herself.

She didn't want to say money.

It felt like a dirty word.

Gloria finished the sentence for her anyway.

"—we don't have money like other people," Gloria said quietly.

Brenda nodded.

Tears spilled.

Gloria reached out and wiped one tear with her thumb.

Then another.

Her hand was warm.

Steady.

"You think I don't know that?" Gloria asked softly.

Brenda sniffled.

Gloria took a breath and looked away for a second, like she was choosing whether to open a door she usually kept shut.

Then she looked back at Brenda.

And she spoke.

Not like a mom brushing hair.

Not like a mom making dinner.

Like a human being.

Like a woman.

Like someone with a past.

"Brenda," Gloria said, voice low, "I didn't grow up with money either."

Brenda blinked.

Gloria nodded, like she was remembering something heavy.

"My mom worked two jobs," Gloria continued. "And my dad… he wasn't around much."

Brenda swallowed.

Her heart squeezed.

She knew that feeling.

Not from memory.

From absence.

Gloria stared down at Brenda and her voice grew even softer.

"I used to watch other girls get things I couldn't," Gloria said. "Pretty dresses. New shoes. Hair done perfect."

Brenda listened like she was hearing a secret story.

Gloria's mouth tightened.

"And I used to feel small," Gloria admitted. "I used to feel embarrassed."

Brenda whispered, "Like me?"

Gloria nodded slowly.

"Like you," she said.

Then Gloria exhaled and smiled—barely.

"But here's the truth," Gloria said. "I wasn't small."

Brenda stared.

Gloria leaned closer.

"I was strong," Gloria whispered. "I just didn't know it yet."

Brenda's tears slowed.

Gloria continued.

"And when I got older," Gloria said, "I promised myself if I ever had a daughter…"

Gloria's voice cracked a little.

"I promised I would never let her feel like she had to shrink just because we didn't have money."

Brenda's chest tightened again.

"Mom…" Brenda whispered.

Gloria kissed her forehead.

"That's why I work," Gloria said. "That's why I pay Doris. That's why I stretch my dollars until they scream."

Brenda let out a shaky laugh through tears.

Gloria laughed too.

A real laugh this time.

Then Gloria's face grew serious again.

"I'm not paying for ballet because you might become famous," Gloria said.

Brenda blinked.

Gloria shook her head gently.

"I'm paying because ballet is teaching you something I never learned as a little girl."

Brenda's voice came out small.

"What?"

Gloria didn't hesitate.

"Confidence," Gloria said.

That word hit Brenda's chest like warmth.

Gloria continued.

"Discipline. Pride. Courage," Gloria said. "And a place where you can belong."

Brenda stared at the floor, breathing slowly.

Gloria lifted Brenda's chin gently with two fingers.

"And I want you to remember this," Gloria said firmly.

Brenda looked into her mom's eyes.

Gloria's eyes shined in the lamp light.

Tired.

But fierce.

"You are not poor," Gloria said. "You are not less."

Brenda's lips trembled.

Gloria squeezed her shoulders.

"You are Brenda Holbul," Gloria said. "And you dance like you mean it."

Brenda's dimples tried to appear, but her face was still too emotional.

She whispered, "I do mean it."

Gloria nodded.

"I know you do."

After that talk, the apartment felt warmer.

Not because the heat changed.

Because Brenda's heart changed.

Brenda finished her practice.

Not perfectly.

But proudly.

And Gloria stood there watching like she wasn't tired anymore.

Like her daughter's determination was recharging her.

When Brenda finished her final bow, she stood still.

Gloria clapped softly.

Not loud.

Just enough.

Brenda smiled.

Dimples finally came.

Then she said something that made Gloria freeze again.

"Mom?"

Gloria smiled. "Yeah?"

Brenda's voice was small but strong.

"Thank you for choosing me."

Gloria's eyes filled instantly.

She covered her mouth with one hand like she was trying to keep a sob from escaping.

Then she pulled Brenda into her chest and hugged her so hard it almost hurt.

"I always choose you," Gloria whispered into Brenda's hair.

"Always."

The next day at ballet, Brenda walked in different.

Her hair still had flyaways.

Her tights were still washed and reused.

Her slippers were still worn.

But she held her head higher.

Not because she was pretending.

Because she finally believed it:

She wasn't less.
She was loved.

And that love was worth more than any rich girl's perfect hair.

Even Clair's.

Even anybody's.

Brenda stepped onto the studio floor with her sisters around her.

With her mother behind her.

With her own name inside her like a shield.

And when Doris clapped and called them to line up…

Brenda didn't feel scared.

She felt ready.

CHAPTER FOURTEEN

Gloria Holbul didn't get visitors.

Not the kind of visitors that knocked like they belonged.

Not the kind of visitors that showed up with a bag in one hand and a whole new energy in the other.

So when the knock came on the door that Saturday afternoon, Gloria paused like her brain had to load the moment first.

Brenda Holbul was sitting on the floor in the living room, tying and untying her worn ballet slippers over and over again like it was a ritual.

Gloria walked to the door cautiously and opened it.

And there he was.

A man standing with his shoulders loose, posture calm, eyes sharp.

He wasn't dressed fancy, but he looked clean.

And his smile—

his smile was bright.

Not because he was happy.

Because his teeth were gold.

Like sunlight trapped in a grin.

"Hey, sis," the man said.

Gloria blinked twice.

Then her hand flew up to her mouth.

"Carl?" she whispered.

Carl's grin widened like it had been waiting years to exist.

"It's me," he said. "I'm here."

Gloria didn't hesitate.

She stepped forward and hugged him hard—so hard Brenda could hear it, like two people holding on tight so the past couldn't pull them apart again.

Brenda stood up slowly, staring.

Gloria pulled back, eyes shiny.

Then she looked at Brenda.

"Brenda," Gloria said gently, "come here, baby."

Brenda shuffled over, confused.

Gloria placed a hand on Carl's arm.

"This is my brother," Gloria told Brenda. "This is your uncle."

Brenda's eyes widened.

She didn't really remember having an uncle.

Not a real one.

Not one that stood in her living room smiling like a movie character.

Carl crouched down to her height.

He smelled like cologne and clean soap and outside air.

"Hey," Carl said softly. "You Brenda?"

Brenda nodded.

"Yes."

Carl smiled again and the gold flashed.

Brenda stared at it like it was treasure.

Carl chuckled.

"I know," he said, amused. "The teeth is a lot."

Brenda didn't know what to say.

So she did what she always did when she felt nervous.

She smiled.

Dimples.

Carl pointed at her cheeks instantly.

"Ohhh," he said, nodding like he'd discovered something important. "You got them dimples."

Brenda giggled.

Gloria exhaled like she hadn't breathed right all week.

For the first time in a while, the apartment felt full.

Not full of money.

Full of people.

Full of warmth.

Later, after Carl put his bag down and sat at the small kitchen table, he looked around like he was taking inventory of the life his sister had built.

Not judging.

Just noticing.

Gloria made coffee she couldn't really afford and poured it into mismatched mugs like it was normal hospitality.

Carl sipped it slow.

Then glanced at Brenda sitting nearby, swinging her legs under the chair.

"So," Carl said, looking at Gloria, "this little one… she really doin' ballet?"

Gloria smiled softly.

"She's been working hard," Gloria said. "Doris says she has presence."

Carl nodded like he respected Doris's opinion even though he'd never met Doris in his life.

Brenda looked up.

"Presence?" Brenda asked.

Carl leaned toward her.

"Presence mean when you walk in a room," Carl said, "and the room gotta pay attention."

Brenda blinked like that sounded dangerous.

Carl smiled.

"That's power," he added.

Gloria shook her head with a little laugh.

"Carl," Gloria warned gently.

Carl held both hands up.

"What?" he said. "I'm just tellin' her the truth."

Then Carl looked at Brenda with a grin.

"Show me something," he said.

Brenda froze.

Her heart jumped.

Show him something?

Gloria touched Brenda's shoulder.

"It's okay," Gloria whispered. "Just show him something Miyla taught you."

Brenda swallowed.

Then she stood up slowly, stepping back onto the living room carpet.

She lifted her arms like Doris taught her—rounded, gentle, controlled.

Then she did the quick twirl Miyla had shown her.

It wasn't huge.

It wasn't perfect.

But it was smooth.

And when she stopped, she held her pose like she meant it.

Conviction.

Carl stared like Brenda had just performed on stage.

Then he smiled wide.

Gold flashing.

He clapped once.

Then twice.

Then he laughed.

"Okayyyy," Carl said, nodding hard. "I see you!"

Brenda giggled, cheeks warm.

Gloria smiled like she wanted to cry but refused to in front of her little girl.

Carl leaned back in the chair.

"She got it," he said.

Gloria's voice was soft.

"She really does."

Later that evening, when Brenda went to her room to play quietly, Gloria and Carl talked in the kitchen in low voices.

That grown-up voice tone.

The one kids aren't supposed to hear.

But kids always hear it anyway.

Gloria didn't say everything.

She didn't dump her whole world on her brother.

But Gloria was tired.

And the way Carl listened…

it made it easier for her to speak.

"We're struggling," Gloria admitted quietly.

Carl didn't flinch.

He nodded like he already knew.

Gloria stared down into her mug.

"I can pay Doris," she said. "Barely. I can keep her in class."

Carl waited.

Gloria's voice cracked just a little.

"But I can't keep up with everything else."

Carl's eyes narrowed.

"Like what?"

Gloria exhaled.

"Food," she said. "Good food. The kind that gives her energy."

Carl nodded slowly.

"And… her tights," Gloria added. "Her stockings. She needs new ones."

Carl stared.

Gloria looked embarrassed even saying it.

"She's growing fast," Gloria whispered. "And the ones she has are… worn."

Carl leaned back in his chair, jaw tight.

The kind of tight that wasn't anger at Gloria.

Anger at life.

Anger at how hard it was for good people to stay afloat.

Carl's voice softened.

"I'm sorry, sis."

Gloria shook her head.

"Don't be," she said quickly. "I'm doing what I can."

Carl nodded.

"I know you are," he said. "I know."

There was a pause.

Then Carl said something Gloria wasn't expecting.

"You know why I came out here?" Carl asked.

Gloria looked at him.

Carl's eyes were serious now.

"No jokes. No shine."

"I been locked up," Carl said. "And I thought about you a lot."

Gloria's throat tightened.

Carl continued quietly.

"In there, you learn respect. You learn what society really is."

He glanced toward Brenda's room.

"You learn what it mean when somebody out here grindin' the right way. Struggling the right way."

Gloria blinked slowly, listening.

Carl sighed.

"I was a dummy," he admitted. "Robbin' a liquor store like I was some kind of genius."

Gloria didn't interrupt.

Carl didn't want sympathy.

He wanted truth.

Carl shook his head once like he still hated his old self.

"I did my time," he said. "And I ain't proud. But I learned."

Gloria stared at him.

"Carl…"

Carl lifted a hand.

"Nah. Let me finish."

Gloria stayed quiet.

Carl leaned forward and lowered his voice.

"Before I got locked up," Carl said, "I bought crypto."

Gloria blinked again.

"Crypto?" she repeated.

Carl nodded.

"Yeah," he said. "I forgot about it almost. But when I got out, I got back into my account."

Gloria waited, unsure where this was going.

Carl smiled again—smaller this time, almost shy.

"I got about forty-eight thousand now," he said.

Gloria's mouth parted slightly.

She didn't even know what to say.

That number didn't sound real.

Carl shrugged.

"Prison time made it grow," he said casually. "Time did what time do."

Gloria stared.

Carl grinned and tapped his gold teeth with his tongue like he was proud of them.

"That's how I bought these," Carl said, laughing.

Gloria finally let out a small laugh too.

But it died quick.

Because Gloria wasn't laughing at the teeth.

Gloria was thinking about Brenda.

About tights.

About food.

About bills.

About how close they were to falling behind.

Carl saw it in her face.

He didn't ask permission.

He didn't wait for pride to get in the way.

He stood up.

"Get her jacket," Carl said.

Gloria blinked. "What?"

Carl smiled.

"We goin' to the ballerina shop."

Brenda came out of her room a few minutes later wearing her little coat.

Her eyes were wide.

"Where we going?" she asked.

Carl winked.

"Somewhere important," he said.

Gloria walked with them, still confused and emotional at the same time.

They drove to the shop in Carl's rental car— nice, clean, smooth.

Brenda sat in the back seat like she was being transported to a new universe.

When they arrived, the ballerina shop looked expensive just from the outside.

Everything in the window was pretty.

Soft colors. Sparkle. Satin. Tulle.

Brenda stepped inside and her eyes lit up like fireworks.

There were racks of tights.

Rows of shoes.

Beautiful outfits.

Everything looked like it belonged to rich kids.

Brenda touched a pair of stockings gently like they might bite.

Carl leaned down.

"Pick what you need," he told her.

Brenda looked up, nervous.

"But… it costs money."

Carl laughed.

"It sure do," he said.

Brenda's voice got quieter.

"I don't want you to spend a lot."

Carl stared at her for a second.

Something shifted in his face.

Like he saw how grown Brenda sounded.

How careful.

How she already carried adult worries in a little kid body.

Carl crouched down again so his face was close to hers.

"Brenda," he said warmly, "listen to me."

Brenda listened.

Carl smiled wide—gold shining.

"That's thug life," Carl said. "We do it for the kids."

Brenda blinked.

She didn't know what thug life meant.

She didn't know what Carl had been through.

She didn't know what kind of regret sat behind that smile.

But she understood the part that mattered.

We do it for the kids.

Brenda smiled.

Dimples.

"Okay," she whispered.

Carl bought Brenda three new sets of stockings.

Not cheap ones.

Good ones.

Soft ones.

The kind that didn't itch.

Then Carl walked her over to the ballet shoes.

Brenda's eyes landed on a pair that looked like royalty.

They were padded.

Thicker in the right places.

Comfortable.

Supportive.

The kind of shoe that looked like it could protect her feet instead of punishing them.

Carl noticed her staring.

"You like those?" he asked.

Brenda nodded slowly.

"They're… really pretty."

Carl waved the worker over.

"We'll take those," Carl said.

Gloria's eyes widened.

"Carl," Gloria whispered, "those are expensive."

Carl didn't even blink.

"She gonna grow out of 'em," Carl said, "but she gonna grow into her confidence first."

Gloria's eyes filled instantly.

She turned her head so she wouldn't cry in public.

But Carl saw anyway.

Carl spoke softer now, so only Gloria could hear.

"She deserve nice things too," he said. "You been holding it down."

Gloria nodded, swallowing hard.

"Thank you," she whispered.

Carl shrugged like it was nothing.

But his voice was low and sincere.

"It ain't nothing," he said. "It's family."

On the way home, Brenda held the bag in her lap like it was full of gold bars.

Because to her…

it was.

It was comfort.

It was pride.

It was proof she wasn't behind.

When she got home, she ran into her room and put on the new shoes.

They fit like a dream.

They didn't pinch her toes.

They didn't rub her heels raw.

They felt like pillows compared to her old cheap pair.

Brenda stood up in them and took a few steps.

Then she twirled.

Smooth.

Clean.

Comfortable.

Her face lit up.

Carl watched from the doorway and smiled like it healed something in him.

Gloria watched too, eyes shining, hand over her mouth.

Brenda looked up at them.

"I feel like… I'm floating," Brenda whispered.

Carl nodded proudly.

"That's what I'm talkin' about," he said.

Brenda hesitated, then said softly:

"Thank you, Uncle Carl."

Carl's gold smile flashed.

He stepped forward and tapped Brenda's chest gently with one finger.

"Don't thank me too much," Carl said, grinning. "Just dance."

Brenda nodded.

Then she hugged him tight.

Carl hugged her back, slow and careful, like he was afraid to break something precious.

And for the first time in a long time…

Gloria's apartment didn't feel like a struggle.

It felt like a home full of love.

Like help had finally arrived.

Like family had finally reached back in.

And Brenda, standing there in her new padded shoes, felt something bloom in her chest.

Not pride.

Not arrogance.

Something cleaner.

Hope.

Because sometimes, in life…

a little support changes everything.

CHAPTER FIFTEEN

Recital day arrived like a storm.

Not a loud storm with thunder and lightning.

A quiet storm.

A storm made of nerves, tight stomachs, shaky hands, and little hearts beating too fast inside tiny ballerina chests.

Brenda Holbul woke up before her alarm.

Her eyes opened in the dark and she just laid there, staring at the ceiling, breathing slow like she was trying to calm her own soul.

Her new ballet shoes sat by the wall like they were waiting.

Clean.

Soft.

Padded.

Like a promise.

Brenda swung her legs out of bed and stood up.

Her feet touched the floor and she didn't feel fear first.

She felt responsibility.

Like today was important.

Like today meant something.

Brenda walked into the kitchen.

Gloria was already there.

Of course she was.

Gloria had coffee in her hand, hair tied back, eyes tired—but bright.

Like she was running on love instead of sleep.

When Gloria saw Brenda, she smiled.

"Good morning, booboo."

Brenda whispered back, "Good morning."

Gloria walked over and hugged her.

Long hug.

No words.

Just warmth.

Then Gloria pulled away and looked her daughter up and down.

"Okay," Gloria said softly. "Let's get you ready."

Brenda's hair looked different today.

Not perfect because of money.

Perfect because of effort.

Gloria brushed it slowly, carefully.

She used the new hair ties she bought on sale.

She smoothed down the flyaways with a wet comb and a prayer.

And for the first time in a long time, Brenda didn't feel embarrassed in the mirror.

She felt beautiful.

Not Barbie beautiful.

Not rich-girl beautiful.

A different kind.

The kind that comes from being cared for.

Gloria tied Brenda's hair tight.

Then kissed her cheek.

"Look at you," Gloria whispered.

Brenda smiled.

Dimples.

"I look like a ballerina," Brenda said.

Gloria's eyes watered.

"You are a ballerina," Gloria corrected.

Brenda nodded slowly, absorbing that truth like it was medicine.

When they arrived at the recital building, Brenda's stomach twisted so hard she thought she might throw up.

The place was bigger than Doris's studio.

Bigger mirrors.

Bigger floors.

Bigger everything.

There were rows of chairs.

A stage.

Curtains.

Bright lights that made the air feel hot.

Parents were everywhere, carrying bags and flowers and cameras like they were soldiers marching into war.

Brenda clutched Gloria's hand.

Gloria squeezed back.

"You okay?" Gloria asked.

Brenda swallowed.

"I'm scared."

Gloria nodded like fear was normal.

"Good," Gloria said. "That means you care."

Brenda whispered, "What if I mess up?"

Gloria crouched down and looked Brenda in the eyes.

"You will mess up," Gloria said honestly.

Brenda blinked, shocked.

Gloria smiled gently.

"And you will still be wonderful," Gloria finished.

Brenda's chest loosened.

She nodded.

"Okay."

Gloria kissed her forehead.

"Go find your sisters," Gloria whispered.

Brenda turned and walked toward the changing area like she was stepping into destiny.

Backstage, the girls looked like tiny angels preparing for battle.

Pink skirts.

White tights.

Hair slicked back.

Cheeks shiny from nervous sweat.

Olga spotted Brenda instantly.

"BRENDA!" Olga squealed.

Brenda ran to her.

Olga grabbed her hands and looked at her feet.

"Oh my God," Olga whispered dramatically. "Those shoes is NICE."

Brenda giggled.

Kisha walked up behind Olga and nodded.

"Okayyy," Kisha said. "Brenda got the deluxe package."

Miyla grinned.

"Let me touch them," Miyla joked.

Brenda laughed.

Then Anastasia waddled in wearing her uniform, hair neat, face glowing like she was pure joy in human form.

Anastasia saw Brenda's shoes and gasped.

"Brenda shoes!" Anastasia yelled proudly like it was her own accomplishment.

Brenda hugged her.

Clair Thompson approached next, quiet and composed.

Clair looked Brenda up and down, then nodded once.

"You look… really good," Clair said.

Brenda blinked.

Clair didn't compliment people often.

Brenda smiled.

"Thank you," Brenda whispered.

Clair's eyes softened.

Then she leaned closer.

"Don't let them scare you," Clair added quietly.

Brenda stared at her.

Clair continued, voice low.

"You dance like you mean it."

Brenda swallowed hard.

Hearing that from Doris was one thing.

Hearing it from Clair?

That meant Brenda had changed the room.

Changed the story.

Brenda nodded.

"I will," she whispered.

Olga clapped her hands together.

"Okay sisters!" Olga shouted. "We about to be famous!"

Kisha snorted. "Girl, we about to be terrified."

Miyla laughed. "Both!"

Anastasia bounced excitedly, chanting wrong as usual.

"Re-sital! Re-sital!"

The girls burst out laughing again.

And that laughter saved Brenda.

Because it reminded her:

This wasn't just pressure.

This was joy.

This was something they earned together.

Then Doris walked in.

Clipboard in hand.

Bun tight.

Old, short, sharp.

But today… even Doris looked different.

Not softer.

Not less strict.

Just… proud.

Doris clapped once.

The girls instantly stood straight.

"Ladies," Doris said.

The giggles died.

The room became still.

Doris paced in front of them slowly.

"You have worked," Doris said. "You have practiced. You have suffered."

Olga whispered, "True," and Kisha elbowed her.

Doris continued.

"Today, you do not dance to be perfect," Doris said.

Brenda's stomach tightened.

Doris's eyes locked onto the group like she was locking them into a spell.

"You dance to be brave," Doris said.

Brenda felt her throat tighten.

Doris stepped closer.

"You dance to show the world what discipline looks like," Doris said.

She paused.

"And you dance for each other."

Brenda blinked fast.

Because suddenly her eyes were watering.

Not fear tears.

Pride tears.

Doris's voice dropped lower.

"Now listen," Doris warned. "Once you step on that stage, you will want to run."

Some girls nodded.

Doris raised her clipboard.

"But you will not run."

The room went dead quiet.

Doris lowered the clipboard.

"You are ballerinas," Doris said simply.

And just like that…

the fear turned into steel.

A staff member peeked in and said, "You're up next."

Brenda's stomach dropped again.

The girls formed their line.

Brenda stood beside Olga and Kisha, with Miyla near the front and Clair near the center.

Anastasia stood a little behind, smiling and breathing hard.

Brenda looked around at them.

Her sisters.

Her team.

Her mirror-room family.

Olga whispered, "We got this."

Kisha whispered, "We don't got this."

Miyla whispered, "We got this."

Clair whispered, "Focus."

Anastasia whispered, "I hungry."

Brenda laughed quietly through her nerves.

Then the curtains opened.

And they stepped onto the stage.

The lights were blinding.

The audience was a sea of faces.

Hundreds of eyes.

Phones raised.

Cameras flashing.

Brenda's breath caught.

For one terrifying second…

she wanted to run off the stage.

She wanted to hide in Gloria's van.

She wanted to disappear back into the safe little dance studio where the mirrors were familiar.

But then she spotted something.

In the front row.

Gloria.

Sitting forward in her chair, eyes shining, hands clasped like she was praying.

Beside her sat Carl.

Gold teeth glowing even in the dim theater light.

Carl lifted both hands and silently mouthed:

You got this.

Brenda swallowed.

Her chest filled with heat.

She turned back forward.

The music began.

Soft at first.

Elegant.

Like a story opening.

Brenda lifted her arms.

First position.

Chin up.

Presence.

The girls moved together.

Four steps.

Pose.

Turn.

Brenda's feet felt different in her new shoes.

She didn't hurt.

She didn't wobble.

She felt supported.

Her confidence rose like water filling a cup.

Olga stayed controlled.

Kisha stayed smooth.

Miyla stayed timed perfectly.

Clair looked like perfection itself.

Anastasia moved slower, but she didn't stop smiling once.

And Brenda…

Brenda danced with conviction.

Not because she wanted applause.

Because she wanted to honor the work.

Honor the bruises.

Honor the struggle.

Honor her mother's tired hands.

Honor her uncle's second chance.

Honor her own heart.

The routine flowed.

And when the moment came for Brenda's turn…

the small front-center pause…

Brenda stepped into it without fear.

She held the pose.

She turned.

She landed it.

And she didn't just look like a ballerina.

She was one.

The music ended.

The girls held their final pose.

The room was silent for half a second.

Then the applause hit like a wave crashing.

Brenda's chest jumped.

The sound was huge.

Warm.

Real.

Olga's smile got massive.

Kisha's eyes widened like she couldn't believe they survived.

Miyla looked like she might cry.

Clair remained calm, but her lips curved into the tiniest proud smile.

Anastasia waved at the audience like she was greeting old friends.

And Brenda…

Brenda felt something she had never felt before.

Not just happiness.

Not just relief.

Victory.

Not over the other girls.

Not over poverty.

Not over mean words.

Victory over herself.

Brenda bowed with the group.

Twelve tiny ballerinas.

One line.

One sisterhood.

And when they bowed…

it felt like the whole world was bowing back.

Backstage, chaos erupted.

Parents waiting.

Hugs.

Flowers.

Pictures.

Voices calling names.

Brenda ran straight to Gloria.

Gloria dropped to her knees and wrapped Brenda up like she was holding her life.

"You did it," Gloria whispered into Brenda's hair. "You did it."

Brenda hugged her mom so tight she could barely breathe.

"I was scared," Brenda admitted.

Gloria pulled back and looked into Brenda's eyes.

"You were brave anyway," Gloria said.

Brenda nodded.

Carl walked up next and crouched down.

He grinned wide.

Gold shining like a trophy.

"That's what I'm talkin' about!" Carl said. "My niece out here shining!"

Brenda giggled.

Carl tapped her shoes with his finger.

"Told you," he said. "Thug life. We do it for the kids."

Brenda laughed again, dimples deep.

"I still don't know what that means," Brenda confessed.

Carl laughed so hard he had to cover his mouth.

Gloria shook her head, smiling through tears.

"It means he loves you," Gloria said.

Brenda looked up at Carl.

Carl nodded seriously now.

"Yeah," Carl said. "It mean I love you."

Brenda's smile softened.

Then she hugged him too.

And Carl hugged her back with both arms, tight and careful, like he was protecting something holy.

That night at home, after the recital was over and the costumes were packed away, Brenda sat on the edge of her bed holding her ballet shoes.

She ran her fingers along the padding again.

She thought about the stage lights.

The applause.

The way her body moved without breaking.

Gloria peeked into the room.

"You okay?" she asked softly.

Brenda nodded.

Then whispered, "I want to keep doing ballet forever."

Gloria smiled.

"I know," she said.

Brenda looked up.

"Even if we don't have money?" Brenda asked.

Gloria walked in and sat beside her.

She brushed Brenda's hair back gently.

"We'll find a way," Gloria whispered. "We always do."

Brenda nodded, sleepy now.

Gloria kissed her forehead.

"Goodnight, ballerina."

Brenda's eyes closed slowly.

"Goodnight, mama."

And just before she fell asleep, Brenda thought about Doris's first day words:

You're sisters now.

Brenda smiled in the dark.

Because she finally understood.

Ballet didn't just teach her how to dance.

It taught her how to stand tall.

How to survive hard things.

How to love people who loved her back.

How to rise after a fall.

And how to bow—
not as a weak little girl—

but as a ballerina.

THE END

Made in the USA
Coppell, TX
12 February 2026